W9-AHM-428

DEFICIT ENDING

. . .

Previous novels by Lee Martin:

Hal's Own Murder Case
Death Warmed Over
Murder at the Blue Owl
A Conspiracy of Strangers
Too Sane a Murder

DEFICIT ENDING

▪ ▪ ▪

▪ *Lee Martin* ▪

St. Martin's Press
New York

 For information, address St. Martin's Press, 175 Fifth Avenue, New York, N.Y. 10010.

Library of Congress Cataloging-in-Publication Data

Martin, Lee.
Deficit ending / Lee Martin.
p. cm.
ISBN 0-312-03813-5
I. Title.
813'.54—dc20 89-24124

First edition

10 9 8 7 6 5 4 3 2 1

This is dedicated, with respect and love, to Laura Taylor, who gave me a bank robbery . . . and for many other reasons of which she is aware.

DEFICIT ENDING

. . .

1

IT IS JUST BARELY possible that somewhere in the universe there might have been someone who was less enthusiastic about returning to work than I was, that Saturday morning in May when the bank robbery went down. Not that I was scheduled to return to work on Saturday. But Monday was looming dismally ahead. I had been on maternity leave since early in March, and Cameron—the baby I had succeeded in producing in a small town in northern New Mexico, about six hours after being involved in what is often known as a Mexican standoff—was proving quite interesting. The idea of returning to the world of holdups and homicides, fingerprints and stakeouts, was not at all enticing.

But with four people, a dog, a cat, a house, a car, and a pickup truck to support, somebody in the family had to have a job and Harry wasn't it. Not anymore. The doctor had just informed us that the chances of his being able to go back to being a helicopter test pilot were exactly zero. Oh, he could still fly his small private plane just fine. But to be able to fly a helicopter you have to do a little better than be able to chew bubblegum and walk at the same time. To be precise, you have to have both feet and both hands doing separate things all at the same time. And to fly new prototype helicopters that maybe were going to turn out not to do quite exactly what they were told to do, you have to be even better than that.

Harry wasn't. Not anymore. Not since February, when a *very* new prototype had done exactly what it was not supposed to do, namely sat down in the middle of a highway. Hard.

On its side.

Now, I would not want to imply that the company wasn't taking care of Harry. It was. Sort of. It was just that it seemed to assume Harry would be drawing Social Security as well as company benefits, but the Social Security people had pointed out quite truthfully that although a minor limp might disable Harry for the job he had been doing, it certainly didn't prevent him from working at another job.

The trouble with that, Harry pointed out to me, loudly and repeatedly, was that he didn't *have* another job. And he didn't *know* another job. He'd been flying helicopters quite a long time. And if you've looked at the economy in Texas lately—well, I don't know where all this famous economic recovery is going on, but it certainly isn't here.

So one of us had to have a job, and it appeared that I was elected. Which meant that my never-fully-formulated plans to quit the police department and stay home with the baby had thoroughly and completely blown up in my face. I had two days left. Monday morning bright and early it was back to the salt mines.

So what was I doing downtown, about seven blocks from the police station, on Saturday morning at nine-thirty?

I was going to the bank, that was what I was doing. The

same bank I had been using for the last fifteen years. The bank that was only about half a block from the old police station, but when the police station moved I didn't exactly want to change banks even though there was a nice new bank only a block from the nice new police station. A creature of habit, that's me.

Not, however, so much of a creature of habit that I had yet resumed wearing the shoulder holster I had worn all the time—even jogging, even going out to dinner—for the last five years, ever since I went into CID, the criminal investigation division. And really it wouldn't have done me much good if I had been wearing it; I certainly was not going to get into a shoot-out with a baby riding on my hip.

Well. I didn't plan to.

But you know that line about the best-laid plans of mice and men? That goes for women too.

This wasn't the full-scale bank, this was only one of those little branch banks that normally have three tellers, and one had gone on vacation. So with another one now on break there was exactly one teller working, and the line stretched somewhat farther than one wants a line to stretch. The lobby—unlike the lobby of a full-scale bank—was small, but as small as it was it had all the appurtenances of a bank. That is, marble. Lots of it. Marble floors, marble counters. You are supposed to be quiet in banks. Sometimes I think banks think they are churches.

Cameron was fussing; I was in the process of switching him over to a bottle, and he was making it plain he did not appreciate the change. So he would fuss and I would offer him the bottle and he would suck on it a swig or two and then sort of push it out of his mouth and fuss some more. Now, one thing about marble, it is noisy. Even with one of those nice baffle-board ceilings, sounds bounced around this room. Any sounds, all sounds. Including, of course, the protests made by an offended baby. By now people had begun to look at me with annoyed expressions, as if I had brought a fussy baby into the bank just to hassle them. I started to point out to some of them that if they objected that much they *could* let me in line ahead of them, but of course I did not really do that because I am a very nice lady.

Then the street door opened again and a couple of men came in together. They pushed their way through the line that had continued to form behind me, and I heard somebody say indignantly, "Hey!"

Or something like hey.

One of the men said, "Shut up." Or something like shut up.

He said it loudly.

It echoed, the sound ricocheting off that marble like a bullet, and everybody looked around. Of course not everybody saw them. At least to judge by the descriptions given later not everybody saw them, but right then it appeared to me that everyone saw them.

I could describe them exactly, and I did, about half an hour later to one of the departmental secretaries. Two white males. One about five-seven and one about six-two. Both of them were wearing ski masks, but I know they were white males because although they were both wearing long sleeves and gloves one of them had, presumably absentmindedly, rolled his sleeves up.

All right, you want to put it that way, I knew that one of them was white. Judging from their voices, I was pretty sure they were both male.

They were both wearing khaki pants and blue plaid work shirts—flannel—and yellowish-tan work boots, and they were both carrying sawed-off shotguns.

Need I mention that I do not like sawed-off shotguns? In fact I don't like any kind of shotguns, but I especially do not like sawed-off shotguns.

So what did I do?

I held very, very still and hoped Cameron would shut up. Which of course Cameron did not do.

He was not the only one. One woman about two people ahead of me in line was screaming like a fire siren. You can imagine what *that* sounded like bouncing off all that marble. It's a wonder they didn't hear her in Dallas.

"Shut up!" the tall one yelled again. "I want everybody on the floor, nice and quiet, and nobody'll get hurt."

He didn't explain whether he wanted us to sit down or lie down. Neither did the other one, who up to this point had not said anything at all. I sat.

Then I thought better of it and lay down, putting Cameron underneath me. If anybody got hurt I didn't want it to be him. If they had rifles or pistols, covering him wouldn't have done any good, but with a scattergun it might. Maybe.

Cameron did not appreciate having me on top of him. He expressed his displeasure loudly.

"Lady, shut that baby up!" the short one yelled.

I shut Cameron up. Not with a bottle. Would you believe some old biddy beside me had the nerve to look shocked?

The tall one vaulted over the counter. I could see where he put his hand flat on that shiny polished marble surface. If he hadn't been wearing gloves that would have been more than sufficient to nail him, if he had any kind of record at all. But as I said he was wearing gloves.

Not everybody was as cooperative as I was; the woman who was screaming kept on screaming, and the woman who was staring disapprovingly at me kept on staring—from a standing position—and I heard one man mutter, "Let's rush him."

Someone needed to bring to his attention the small likelihood of anyone short of Superman outrunning a shotgun blast.

"I said *sit down!*" the tall one yelled, and I could hear fraying edges of hysteria in his voice. He wasn't far short of using that shotgun now, whether he'd come in with that in mind or not.

Somebody had to take command or somebody was

going to get killed, and it was pretty evident that he couldn't, even with a shotgun.

So I sat up, still nursing Cameron, and yelled, "You idiots *do what he says!*"

The tall one turned to look at me—I could see his eyes; they were blue—and the short one said, in a very sarcastic tone, "Thank you, lady."

That woman was *still* screaming. I stood up long enough to grab her and sit her down beside me hard. She stopped screaming and started crying. That was preferable, as it was at least quieter, but it wasn't very preferable. She was right in my ear and she wasn't enough quieter to keep from spooking the robbers.

My trained and unshut-offable cop brain went on registering details, mechanically.

The tall one was scooping money out of the teller's drawer and stuffing it into a grocery sack he had with him. One of those white plastic sacks that you carry with the little handles. It was a Winn-Dixie sack.

The short one was shifting back and forth from one foot to the other, as if he had to go to the bathroom. The main thing I could see about him was his feet. He had about the same shoe size as Harry, about a ten. "Let's get out of here," he said nervously.

The tall one went on grabbing money. Evidently he didn't trust the teller to do it herself; there might have been a dye bomb in the drawer, and if he got the money himself he could make sure the dye bomb didn't get into the sack.

He could also make sure nobody hit the bank alarm.

For all the good not hitting the bank alarm was going to do. This was a small branch bank, as I have said; what I did not say was that it was located in a large office building that stays busy even on Saturday. Sure, they try to make these places reasonably soundproof, but no soundproofing was meant to protect against the female fire siren now sitting beside me sobbing. No, nobody was going to hear her now, but it was about a hundred percent certain somebody had heard her earlier; somebody somewhere in that building had by now called the police.

And if somebody inside the building hadn't, somebody passing by on the street probably had. Of all banks to rob, these idiots had picked a branch bank that had storefront windows. The windows were neatly protected from burglary with little strips of burglar alarm tape, but that did nothing to reduce the visibility of this lobby to bystanders.

So almost certainly police cars were en route, even if I hadn't heard sirens yet. Most likely the dispatcher had instructed responding officers not to use sirens. That shouldn't have been necessary. Experienced officers would know it.

But then there are a lot of things experienced officers would know that I couldn't count on the responding officers to know.

Just for example, an experienced police officer would have sense enough to stand back and let the robbers get clear of the building. We are taught—we all are taught, and if we aren't taught we ought to pick it up from fellow officers—that we elected to take the risks, but we don't have the right to inflict the risks on the civilians. If somebody tried to take them while they were still in here, this was going to turn into a hostage situation, and a hostage situation is a lot more dangerous than letting two bank robbers leave the building and trying to pick them up later. Dirty Harry notwithstanding, you don't get into a firefight inside a bank or on the street outside if there is any way you can possibly avoid it.

I didn't have much of a hope that the first officer to respond was going to be experienced. Fort Worth is not exactly the best-paying police department in the universe, and morale goes up and down, up and down. So there is a lot of turnover. And unfortunately some of the people who do stay I would not wish on a dog.

I also didn't have much of a hope that we were dealing with professional criminals here. It would have been better if we were, because pros are a lot less likely to panic and start shooting. There was a time, I am told, when bank robbery was the elite of crime, when bank robbers, like forgers, *did* tend to be pros. It was drugs that changed the rules for bank robbers, just as the offset press changed the rules for forgers. But the difference was that the offset press made forgery easier. Drugs didn't make bank robbery easier; they didn't make bank robbery safer, for either the criminals or the victims. In fact they made it more dangerous. A lot more dangerous.

A lot more dangerous, and a lot more common. For every Butch Cassidy or Jesse James there had been in the past, there were now a hundred, a thousand, hopped-up or crashing kids who needed money to pay the pusher, fast before the last fix wore off.

You don't mess with them. Not if you can get out of it. Especially not with a bank full of civilians.

Was I thinking that, while the robbery was going on and I was trying to keep my baby quiet and safe? You bet I was, because what that first officer on the scene did might make the difference between life and death for my baby and me, or for any one or more of this whole room full of very frightened people.

"Let's get *out* of here!" the short one yelled again. And this time the tall one seemed to hear him.

He vaulted back over the counter. Then he turned, leveling his gun menacingly at the closest person. "Nobody move for five minutes," he said, and the two headed for the door.

Too late.

There was a rookie outside. It had to be a rookie, because nobody else would have had the black-and-white marked car double-parked on the street directly in front of the front door of the bank.

The tall one put out his arm and caught the short one just in time to keep him from going out onto the street. And then, slowly, the two backed inside the room again.

Senior officers are trained to handle hostage situations. Patrolmen aren't. Perhaps the robbers knew that; perhaps that was why they did not wait for a senior officer to arrive. Instead, one of the robbers turned to the teller and said, "Lady, get your car keys."

Mechanically the teller—a young woman in a green dress; she couldn't have been over twenty-five at the very most, and she looked younger—picked up her purse from the floor under the counter, which was an odd place for her to keep it in a bank.

"Just the keys," the short man said. "Not the bag. Leave the bag."

She put the bag on the counter and started to open it. The tall man shoved her aside, opened the bag, and snatched out a set of keys dangling from an orange puff like a psychedelic bunny tail.

And the two robbers and the teller left the bank together. One robber had his gun jammed in the teller's side; the other was walking sideways to guard their backs. And all the patrolman outside, and I inside, could do was sit and watch them go.

The teller never said a word. But she looked at me as she left. I shall never, so long as I live, be able to forget the expression on her face. Because *I* was the one who yelled at everybody to settle down and do as the robbers said. It would have made matters worse—a whole lot worse—if any of the half-baked schemes of any of the would-be heroes who'd wanted to jump the robbers had been tried. I knew that; probably she knew it. But that didn't help either of us. Because she knew, as I knew, that the statistics on live return of hostages aren't very good.

After they left there was a concerted rush for the two doors of the branch bank, the one onto the street and the one into the main part of the building. The patrolman blocked the street door, I blocked the other, juggling my badge and my baby and saying "You can't leave now. We've got to get statements from everybody."

"Deb, you're on it," Captain Millner said to me.

I stared at him with as much indignation as I could

muster. "What do you mean, I'm on it? I'm not due back at work until Monday."

"Tough," he said.

"And I've got a baby with me—"

"Hand her to a secretary."

"Him," I growled. "Can't you tell a boy when you see—"

"Deb," Millner said, "shut up."

By now several FBI agents had arrived, including Dub Arnold, with whom I have worked before. Dub had a rookie in tow again. He frequently does; apparently he is considered a good trainer of rookies. This rookie looked Chinese and his name was Donald Chang. The FBI has come a long way from the days when all its agents were WASP males, but still the agents somehow manage to look cut out with the same cookie cutter even if the cookies now are different sizes and colors. It's because they dress alike, I think, and because of the way they all are trained to think alike.

Donald Chang had never worked a bank robbery before and of course he was getting in the way very badly. After I yelled at him for putting his hand down exactly where we hoped to find the glove print of the robber, Dub crooked a finger at him and said, "Come 'ere, Chang," and they had a quiet conversation in the corner.

Chang returned looking very subdued and asked me, "What else did they touch?"

Dub would not have chewed him out in public, of course, but by this time the witnesses had all been removed by car to the police station to provide statements—not that any of us, including Millner, expected anybody to have seen anything I did not see. The only people left inside the bank were Captain Millner and me, the two FBI agents, our crime scene people, and Tony Winston, the branch manager, who had returned from lunch to discover his teller—Dorene Coe, he said her name was—missing and his bank in the hands of the police. As far as I was concerned there was nothing further to do in the building, and I was ready to leave as soon as Harry, who had been telephoned by the dispatcher, arrived to retrieve his son, which he did while I was talking to Donald Chang.

When Harry arrived he had my shoulder holster and service revolver with him, packed neatly in a brown paper grocery sack. He handed the sack over and collected Cameron, and while he was tucking the baby into his safety seat I was donning the shoulder holster.

Of all the trade-offs I have ever made in my life, I think that was my least favorite.

The sad fact was that we might as well have left the bank the same time the witnesses did; there was nothing worth doing inside the building. We were going through the motions and that was all. They hadn't taken the bait money; Winston was sure of that. The dye bomb hadn't been touched. The serial numbers were unavailable. The robbers had touched the counter and a couple of door frames, but they were definitely wearing gloves, and while it is often possible to identify glove marks it certainly isn't possible to search them as you can latent fingerprints from a crime scene. After Winston took the videotape out of the monitor and gave it to us, all of us—city police and FBI agents, followed by a mob of reporters with video cameras of their own—proceeded over to the police station to view the tape.

Which looked just about as these tapes usually look. I couldn't have been sure of recognizing these robbers if they lived next door to me.

There was considerable commotion in our new, already overcrowded detective bureau. The secretaries can take only so many statements at a time, and they aren't allowed to do it alone because legally the statement is made to a police officer. So we had four detectives from robbery/theft division sitting with four secretaries questioning four witnesses, while all the other witnesses—I counted eleven more—sat in the hall. They were not supposed to be discussing the robbery.

If you believe they were not discussing the robbery, I

would like to sell you some nice oceanfront property in Arizona.

As far as I was concerned robbery/theft ought to be working this robbery. I could not see any earthly reason why it should be my job. I belong to the major case squad, and besides that I'd been off duty for several months. Surely robbery/theft could—

"You were there," Millner reminded me, and that was the end of that.

There was a young man sitting on the floor in the hall who hadn't, so far as I remembered, been inside the bank building. "Who's he waiting for?" I asked the receptionist, a recently hired young woman named Millie. She was the first Millie I had ever known.

"He's a witness," she said. "He was outside. He's the one who called us. He saw them going into the building."

I sat down on the floor beside him, as my office was currently full of people getting statements. "What's your name?" I asked.

"What's yours?" he replied, not too amiably.

I pulled out my badge case. "I'm Deb Ralston, Major Case Squad. Now what's your name?"

"Bengt Daniels," he said, "and I'm a teaching fellow at TCU and I'm supposed to be teaching a class right now."

"So your students get a walk. I'm sure they won't mind."

"The *school* might," he said gloomily.

"Actually TCU is quite good about cooperating with the police department," I assured him. "Let's get out of this commotion."

"Okay by me." He stood up, at which time I could see that his blue jeans, mostly white from fading rather than acid (or glacier) washing, had frayed holes in the knees, and his sandals looked homemade.

TCU is not a low-cost school. His attire was more likely to be Making a Statement than announcing poverty.

On the other hand if he was on a teaching fellowship,

and living on his stipend, the jeans might have come from Goodwill. I am very bad about generalizing.

And right now I would much rather generalize about TCU students than about the probable life expectancy of a bank teller who had gone out the door looking at me.

I led him into a small conference room, which is the room that was called the interrogation room in the days when a cleaning technician was called a janitor, and he looked around with some interest before throwing his book bag on the scarred table and sitting down.

"Now, you are the man who called in the first report of the robbery," I said.

"So they tell me. I can't figure out why some more people didn't. I mean, you don't normally see men with guns going into a bank building."

"You also don't normally see men with guns walking around on the Fort Worth streets," I pointed out. "Did they arrive on foot?"

"No. They had a car. Some woman let them out. I guess she picked them back up but I was on the phone. Didn't that cop—police officer that was standing out front tell you?"

"Not yet he didn't," I said. "What can you tell me about the car?"

"It was red."

I waited. Surely he could tell me something more than that.

He didn't know the make or the model. But he had written down its license plate number, which might or might not be accurate—I had been given a lot of good license plate numbers by cooperative witnesses in the past, but I also had been given a lot of license plate numbers that had been misread, or miscopied, by overexcited witnesses.

Anyway I took the number out in the hall to hand to the receptionist for her to call it down to the communications center—dispatch has a new name—so they could run it on the computer. But I was temporarily sidetracked. Another man got off the elevator. He was tall, slim, and not exactly young. "Where the hell is my wife?" he shouted.

Winston, who was sitting in the hall with the witnesses, came to his feet fast. "Now, Mr. Coe—"

"Don't 'Now Mr. Coe' me!" the man shouted. "I want to know what is being done to find—"

"Mr. Coe, I'm Deb Ralston—" I began.

He glared at me. "I don't want to talk to a secretary, I want to talk to a *cop!*"

"Mr. Coe, I *am* a cop. I'm Detective Deb Ralston and I'm working this case. Would you come in here please?" I opened the door to another conference room and quickly, as he entered it, I handed the plate number to Millie. "Call dispatch and have them run this for registration."

Mr. Coe sat down hard. "What's going on?" he asked me. "What the hell's going on? Sarah Kane called and told me somebody kidnapped my wife."

It took a minute for me to remember that Sarah Kane was the other teller, the one who'd been on break when the robbery went down. "I'll tell you all I know," I said, mentally cursing the men for cowardice. They've gotten to where they *always* leave somebody hysterical for the women to deal with. They *could* have talked to Coe. Or maybe I was being unfair. I had walked up to him myself. "After that I need to get some information from you."

I told him what we knew so far, which was just about exactly nothing except that Dorene Coe had been abducted at gunpoint about two hours earlier by two armed men. I told him we had as much of a lookout as we could place with that little information, and now I needed some information from him. To start with, I needed a good picture of his wife. The bank had a picture but it wasn't a very good one.

They should have done better than that. We had been holding seminars about bank robberies, and they were supposed to have good, clear, current photographs of all their employees in case of this very type of situation. But whoever was supposed to have taken good, recent, clear photographs of Dorene Coe had slipped up. All that was in her file was the second copy of the Polaroid that had gone on her ID card.

Coe dug a picture out of his billfold and gave it to me. It wasn't much better. "This looks like a school picture," I said.

"It is."

"You don't have anything more current?" I asked. The teller had looked young, but surely she wasn't this young.

"How old do you think Dorene is?" he asked tiredly. "Are you judging by my age? Because if you are you're making a mistake. I'm thirty-one. Dorene's nineteen. And don't ask me what I was doing marrying a nineteen-year-old because I damn well don't want to explain it again, especially not to a cop. I just want my wife back. That picture's one year old. She hasn't changed."

"What kind of car does she drive?"

"A Chrysler New Yorker. White. Three months old." Reading my expression correctly, he added, "She doesn't have to work. She wants to work. She says she's not old enough to stay at home all the time. Damn it, she could have gone to college!" He put his head down on the table, face hidden in his arms.

"Mr. Coe, do you know the license plate number?"

His voice muffled, he gave me a license plate number that, like the one I'd gotten from Daniels, might or might not be accurate.

"Where does she keep the car parked when she's at work?"

The parking garage on Main, kitty-cornered across from the bookstore. She rented a slot by the month.

"Thank you, Mr. Coe," I said. "If you don't mind, I'm going to leave you in here where the press can't get at you while I go to check on a few things."

"Go ahead." His voice was still muffled; I think he was crying and didn't want me to see him.

As I shut the door behind me, Captain Millner said, "He settle down any?"

"Yeah," I said. "For now anyway."

"You know who he is, don't you?"

I shook my head. "Am I supposed to?"

He looked at me pityingly. "Deb, don't you ever read the newspapers? He's the guy that runs Coe Electronics. That guy that used to be a teacher but they threw him out of teaching and so he went out and invented that new videotape process."

I must still have looked blank, because Millner went on explaining. "From what I hear, the money he's made in the last two years would make J.R. Ewing look like small change."

· 2 ·

"It's a new process," Millner went on. "The change is in the tape rather than in the VCR, so it doesn't obsolete current equipment but it does get a whole lot better picture."

"And he invented it. I thought the Japanese invented everything like that."

"The Japanese invented a different process. Theirs changes the equipment. Deb, don't you *ever* read the newspaper?"

"When," I asked, "would I get time to read the newspaper? Okay, so the man's got money. What does that have to do with this crime?"

"Just this," Millner said, sitting on the corner of my desk. "There's always the possibility that the robbery wasn't the primary crime."

"What are you talking about?"

"There's always the possibility," Millner said patiently,

"that the real crime was to kidnap Robert Coe's wife, and the robbery was just the cover."

"You weren't there," I said. "I was. They were headed out the door when that running dumb ass parked the prowl car outside. Now look, I've got Coe in one room and Daniels in another. Can somebody else *please* go talk to Coe? I can't talk to them both at once and I'd really rather not talk with Coe."

Captain Millner allowed as how he would go talk to Coe, and I went back to Daniels. Who had his book bag open and his feet on the desk. He was reading *Beowulf,* which strikes me as something nobody would read voluntarily, although I am told that people do. He put the book bag down and looked at me politely as Millie, at the door, said, "Deb?"

And handed me a small piece of paper with an automobile registration written on it.

"Could the red car have been a Buick Regal?" I asked.

He shrugged. "It could have been. I told you I don't know."

"Maybe about an eighty-seven?"

"That sounds about right. It wasn't very old."

I handed the piece of paper back to Millie. "Add this to the lookout. Now, about the woman who was driving—"

He shook his head. "I'm not even sure it was a woman."

"But you said—"

"I know what I said, but I've been thinking and I'm not sure it was a woman. It was somebody with long sandy-blond hair. The person was wearing a red T-shirt. That's really all I saw. I'm sorry if I misled you because I didn't mean to. I just thought it was a woman because of the hair but now I'm not sure it was. Can I go now?"

I got his address and telephone number and let him go. I'd pick him back up later for a written statement. Right now the place was chaos, and I had a lead I wanted to follow up.

University Chrysler-Plymouth. That was the registered owner of the license plate number he'd given me, and I was curious enough about that to sit down at my desk to make some telephone calls.

So I sat down at my desk and the telephone rang. "You know that New Yorker you wanted a patrolman to go look for?" said a male voice with dispatch noises behind it.

"Yeah, I know that New Yorker. What about it?"

"It's gone from the parking garage. The attendant said a man went and got it for Mrs. Coe about two hours ago."

"What sort of a man?"

"He didn't notice."

Well, why should he notice? People pick up cars for other people all the time. If he had her car keys to start the car, and if he had her code to get out of the parking garage, there was no reason at all that the attendant should pay any attention. But that didn't help my mood any, as I hung up and dialed the code for an outside line, to call University Chrysler-Plymouth.

The first person I talked with informed me they had several '87 Buick Regals on their used car lot and was I interested in any special one? It took awhile to get across the fact that I was a police officer and yes indeed I was interested in a special one. After another round or two of cross questions and crooked answers I decided for the good of my temper and blood pressure I'd be better off driving out there.

You know that horrible intersection where Camp Bowie splits off University? I spent five minutes at that traffic light. Well, maybe it wasn't five minutes, but it certainly felt like it. If I had not been so boxed in by traffic that I couldn't have gotten out anyway, I would have been very strongly tempted to get my little bubblegum machine out of the glove box, set it on the dash, plug it in to the cigarette lighter, and turn on my siren. But I wouldn't have been able to move without fifteen cars in front of me moving so I decided it wasn't worth the trouble.

But the trip itself, fortunately, was worth the trouble. The Buick Regal—bright red, right license plate number—was sitting on the lot, with ignition keys in it, and as I stood and looked at it a woman strolled up and said, "I can make you a good deal on that one."

I introduced myself, and she said, "I'm Connie Daynes. I'd be glad to let you take it on a test drive."

"Has somebody else test-driven it today?" I asked. "Maybe kept it out awhile? Somebody with long blond hair and a red T-shirt?"

She looked startled. "Why, yes. Is something wrong? It hasn't been in an accident, has it? Surely I would have noticed—" She looked over at the car, her expression alarmed.

"No accident. Has anybody else driven the car since that person brought it back?"

"No. I was just getting ready to move it. She left it in a ridiculous place, but—"

"So it was a woman?"

"Mrs. Ralston, will you please tell me what's going on?"

So I told her.

When I got through, she shook her head and said, "Well. What do you want me to do now?"

"The car is going to have to be processed for fingerprints," I said, "and I need to get some information from you."

"Fingerprint powder? I had a burglary at my house one time and they got fingerprint powder all over everything. It made a horrible mess. I'm afraid I can't let you—"

"We can, of course, get a search warrant—"

"Oh, dear," she said indecisively, and turned around as if looking for guidance from elsewhere. "I don't know what to—"

"Perhaps you'd better get your manager," I suggested.

"Perhaps I'd better. Can you come with me?"

"I'm going to stay here beside the car."

"We could just lock it up and leave it—"

"I can't do that," I said patiently. "As of this moment, this car is going to be under police surveillance until after it has been fingerprinted."

"Oh, dear," she said again. "Well, I'd better go get Jeff—"

She dithered off, returning a moment later with a tall fellow with a bushy mustache. He was wearing a gray suit, a white shirt, a gray print tie, and looked altogether as if he had been reading Molloy of *Dress for Success* fame.

"I'm Jeff Hardy," he said. "What seems to be the problem?"

"The problem seems to be that this vehicle was borrowed from your lot to be used in a robbery," I said. "A woman has been taken hostage. It is imperative that we fingerprint the car as soon as possible. If we can't do it with your consent then we'll do it without your consent, under a search warrant, but that would waste a lot of very important time."

"But it's going to mess up the upholstery," the saleswoman protested.

"Ms. Daynes, I don't think you understood me," I said softly. "The robbers have taken a hostage. She's nineteen years old. If we don't get her back fast they'll certainly kill her, if they haven't done so already. Any possible lead—"

"Will you do the fingerprinting yourself?" Hardy asked.

"No, I'll be calling our crime scene people to do it."

"Get them on out here. Connie, please help the police all you can." Hardy turned and walked back up the lot.

I returned to the green unmarked police Ford, which I had parked a few feet away from the Buick, and called dispatch. Assured that Irene Loukas from ident would be en route momentarily, I returned to Connie Daynes. "I'll probably need to take you to headquarters later to get a complete statement," I said, "but for now I want to get all the information I can. To start with, let's get a description of the woman who rented the car. Did she drive in, or walk in?"

"Drove."

"So while she was out allegedly test-driving this car

were you looking over her car as a possible trade-in?" I knew she would have been. That is SOP—standard operating procedure.

"Yes, of course I looked at it," Daynes said, not to my surprise.

"Did you fill out one of those sheets you fill out on trade-ins?"

"I filled it out part of the way. You don't finish them unless the person looks like agreeing to the deal."

"Good," I said. "Would you get me what you have?"

"Sure, I can do that." She headed toward the building. I would have liked to have gone with her—this conversation we were having would have been more comfortable indoors, sitting down—but obviously I could not leave the suspect vehicle until somebody arrived to relieve me.

Connie Daynes returned with a clipboard, a partially filled-out form on it. Her handwriting was not the world's neatest, but I was able to determine that the possible trade-in vehicle was a blue 1985 Mercury Lynx, not in very good shape.

She hadn't written down its VIN—vehicle identification number.

She hadn't written down its license number.

Do you know how many Mercury Lynxes—and Ford Escorts, which is exactly the same thing—there are on the road? Do you know how many of them are blue? I've sometimes wondered if they come in any other color without a special order.

I asked, without much hope, whether she had written down the license plate number elsewhere. I might as well have not asked. The answer was exactly what I expected it to be.

"Now let's get to the woman," I said. "She's blond, what else can you tell me about her?"

Connie Daynes shrugged. "I meet so many people."

"I'm sure you do. But this was only a couple of hours ago—"

"Actually it wasn't."

"What?"

"She was here when we opened at nine. She told me she wanted to take the Buick to that diagnostic place on Camp Bowie and have them check it with all those electronic gadgets to see if it needed work. She said it would take probably a couple of hours, maybe a little longer."

That explained how the car had stayed out long enough for a robbery. Normally when I want to buy a car I am allowed to test-drive it around the block with the salesperson with me, and I had been rather wondering how one had stayed out this long. "And you let her take it. Isn't that rather unusual?"

"Mrs. Ralston, I'm paid on a commission basis and I haven't sold a car all month. Yes, it was rather unusual. But I need the money."

"So she took the car—what time?"

"It was around nine-fifteen."

"Didn't you feel a little nervous letting her take it that long?" I asked.

"Not really," Daynes said. "I mean, after all, I had her car."

"All right, so she took the car around nine-fifteen. When did she return it?"

"That was what was funny," Daynes said. "I don't know."

"But you must have had her car keys—"

"I did. I still do. She must have another set. I was talking to somebody else and I looked out around eleven forty-five and saw her car was gone and ours was back."

"So you've still got her keys?"

"That's what I said. I figured she'd come back for them sooner or later. Do you want me to go get them?"

"Not now." The chances that any of the suspect's fingerprints would be left, not covered or wiped out by Connie Daynes's subsequent handling of the keys, were about zero, but about zero does not mean completely zero. It was at least worth trying. So I would wait until Irene got through fingerprinting the Buick and then Irene would take possession of that set of keys. "So you didn't see her come back," I said.

"Uh-uh."

"When she came to get the car was she alone?"

"Yes. She's always been alone."

"Always?" I demanded. "You mean she's been here before?"

"Two or three times. Three I guess. She's been telling me she's definitely going to buy a car and she's been here looking before."

Getting to know you. Getting you used to trusting her. Setting this up. But I know car salespeople fairly well. "If she's been hanging around like that surely you must know her name?"

"She told me it was Melanie Griffith. But I never saw a driver's license or any registration papers or anything like that, so she could have been—"

"Lying. Indeed she could have. All right, let's get on to appearance. What did Melanie Griffith look like?" I had my notebook out by now.

"She was about my height—"

Five feet six inches, I wrote after a fast glance.

"A little thinner than me, not much—"

Hundred and twenty-five pounds.

"Eyes—" She shook her head. "I think they were blue but I'm not going to swear to it. I don't think she's a natural blond but she might be. Fair skin. Light enough she could be natural blond but—you know how natural blonds have hair that is sort of several different colors a little bit different but almost alike? Well, hers was all the same shade. So I think she'd helped it along some."

That, I thought, was something a man wouldn't have noticed. So I was glad I was talking with a woman.

"How was she dressed?" Not that a clothing description would be much help; she'd certainly changed her clothes and possibly her hair color since the robbery, even if she didn't think we knew she was involved.

"Red T-shirt, black slacks. I didn't really notice her

shoes or purse. I think it might have been a straw purse but I'm not sure. Sandals or sneakers. I don't suppose that's much help."

"Age?"

"Oh, I don't know. Thirty, thirty-five."

"Do you think you could recognize her if you saw her again?"

"Oh, yes, certainly."

"Even if her hair was a different color?"

At this Connie Daynes looked uncertain, but then she nodded. "I think so. Probably."

"Then we may be asking you, a little later, to look at some pictures." *And to work with our ident people on a composite drawing,* I thought but did not say. People generally protest when asked to work on a composite; once they get into it they get very interested and very cooperative.

A brown van was turning into the lot. Irene Loukas got out in the gray coveralls she's taken to wearing lately. She says it makes more sense to wear coveralls all the time than to try to wear civilian clothes and ruin them with fingerprint powder. Remembering when I worked in ident, I can certainly see that reasoning, but I'm not used to the coveralls yet. They look kind of funny to me.

Irene climbed back in, and then out of the truck, which was rather too high off the ground for her. She was carrying a clipboard as she came over to me. "Tell me about it," she invited.

So of course I told her about it. I was getting a little tired of telling this story. Not that I was likely to be able to stop telling it any time soon.

She went back to the truck and returned with a camera. She began just as I would have begun when I was in ident, by taking photographs all around the car, one of the front, one of the back, and one of each side. Then she fingerprinted the driver's door carefully before opening the door.

There were no usable prints on the outside of the car

door, and that said a little something. Because normally there will be palm prints on the outside of the door. No, not on the door handles, there's almost nothing usable there at any time because the hand always grasps it the same way and the prints cancel each other out. But on the door itself—

Nothing here. Somebody had wiped the side of the door with a towel. The prints of the towel were quite obvious.

There's one other place you nearly always find prints, and Irene headed for it next. That's the rearview mirror, and that's a place a lot of clever criminals don't think of cleaning. They forget they have touched it. It's sort of an instinct, you get in the car and you adjust the rearview mirror, and often you don't even notice you are doing it.

Somebody had adjusted the rearview mirror in this car. Somebody had left a neat, rather small, piece of palm print on it, the area just below the fingers. It probably wouldn't be possible to search it—it is next door to impossible to make a nonsuspect ident from palm prints—but it would certainly be identifiable if and when we caught up with "Melanie Griffith." In the unlikely event that Melanie Griffith really was her name, and we already had palm prints on file, we could make her fast.

"Melanie Griffith"—whoever she actually turned out to be—had borrowed the car. But we had one witness who had seen both robbers get out of the car. That said there was at least a possibility that both robbers—and the victim—had gotten into the same car; in fact, it was not only possible, it was even likely, because we knew that a man had gone to pick up the victim's car, and the chances that they had marched her around the downtown area at gunpoint were pretty close to nil. Bengt Daniels thought they'd left in the same car they arrived in. But he hadn't been sure.

So Irene fingerprinted the passenger's door, inside and out, as she had done the driver's door. And both backseat doors, inside and out. She printed the seat belt latches.

She printed every hard surface in the car, including the inside of the back window.

The piece of palm print from the rearview mirror was the only print in or on the car. And that said a lot.

Then, with my assistance, she started pulling out the backseat to look behind and under it.

As I said, we give seminars to bank employees on what to do in this kind of situation. One of the instructions they get is to touch everything they possibly can in order to leave their fingerprints and palm prints; these prints are of course on record in the bank (and on that the bank hadn't slipped up. We had Dorene Coe's prints). We also tell them if possible to slip off something identifiable—ring, watch, something of that sort—and slip it down behind the seat, if they can do it without being observed. Of course there was no particular reason to assume that Dorene Coe would have remembered those instructions—she was, after all, only nineteen and certainly very badly frightened—but there was always the possibility.

Somebody had slipped an ornately carved bangle bracelet behind the seat. It looked to me like solid gold.

Dorene Coe had the money to own a solid gold bangle bracelet. I very much doubted that anybody else who would be riding in the backseat of a used car was likely to be in the same financial condition.

Irene photographed the bracelet and then sealed it in a plastic bag; this she would take back into the police station to be fingerprinted.

With Irene working on the Buick, I could leave it now. So I went in and borrowed a phone and a private place to talk from, and called Captain Millner to ask about the bracelet.

We hadn't, of course, needed to ask for a description of Dorene Coe's clothing; I'd seen her myself. But we'd asked all the same, to be sure the descriptions jibed. Even an experienced cop is likely to get rattled in the type of situation I was in. But apparently I hadn't been too rattled, because the husband, the branch manager, the teller who'd been on break when the robbery went down, and I all agreed that Dorene had been wearing a solid green jersey dress (silk jersey, her husband said) with long sleeves, a full skirt, and a jewel neckline. She'd had a green silk paisley scarf draped over her left shoulder, tucked at the waist into a pale-green leather belt. She had on one good necklace, a completely simple cobra chain with no pendant or anything like that on it.

I hadn't had a chance to notice watches, rings, other jewelry. The teller who'd been on break told whoever talked with her that Dorene had been wearing a watch, bracelet, and wedding ring. It wasn't so much that she'd noticed the jewelry that particular day, she added, as it was the fact that Dorene always wore those pieces and no other jewelry.

Millner told me Robert Coe had said Dorene would be wearing a Seiko watch, yellow gold, a two-inch-wide 18-karat gold bangle bracelet with a hand-carved leaf pattern on it, and a gold wedding band, wide and completely plain. She wore no other rings; she had a nice engagement ring but didn't like to wear it because she complained that the Tiffany setting caught on everything.

Robert Coe, Millner added, was still in the police station, pointedly ignoring all polite suggestions that he could now go home.

I took custody of the bracelet and headed for the police station myself.

By now it was almost five o'clock, and I was feeling—physically—like a sadly neglected milch cow. Emotionally I was a wreck, because I could not get rid of the expression on the face of that girl as she went out the door. I felt guilty because I was neglecting my baby, who undoubtedly had been howling for at least the last two hours. I felt guilty because I was neglecting my family; either Harry and our teenager Hal had given up on my prompt return and stuck a pizza into the oven, or else they were sitting patiently waiting for me to come home and make supper. I felt guilty about wanting to go home knowing that somewhere, somewhere, somewhere, Dorene Coe was dead, or else she was alive and waiting without too much hope to be rescued.

I reminded myself that my first partner, Clint Barrington—that was before he went over to the sheriff's office—used to tell me I couldn't save the world and shouldn't go around trying to. It didn't help now any more than it did when Clint first said it.

Coe was still in the interview room or whatever that room is called today. He was a tall man, taller than Harry and thin almost to the point of gauntness, and his graying hair was disheveled. He looked up when I opened the door, and then said, "Oh, it's you."

"Yes. I needed to check with you about something." I didn't usually feel this awkward talking with the family of a victim. But then I wasn't usually quite as closely involved with the crime as I was with this one.

"Well, what?" His voice was neutral.

I put the bracelet, encased in the clear vinyl evidence bag, on the table in front of him.

He picked it up and looked at it. "Where did you get it?"

"Is it Dorene's?"

"Yes, of course it's Dorene's. Where did you get it? Is she—" His voice was rising.

"We haven't found her," I said quickly, and told him where we had gotten the bracelet.

"Now, why would she do that?" he asked. "Why would she take it off? I bought her that in Paris, on our honeymoon. She never takes it off—"

"She's keeping her head," I said softly. "Your wife is a very smart lady. She's trying to leave a trail for us. Without this, we couldn't be a hundred percent certain that was really the getaway car. Now we can be sure. She's keeping her head."

"That doesn't mean they won't kill her."

"No," I agreed, "it doesn't. But if she's staying calm it'll help them stay calm. It means she's got more chance, a lot more chance, than she'd have if she were panicking."

"So what now?" he asked.

"There will be descriptions and photos of her, descriptions and videotapes of the robbery suspects, on the television news and in the papers," I said. "With luck, somebody will recognize somebody. In the meantime, we follow the routine."

"Follow the routine. Is that all?"

"I hear you're an inventor," I said. "How do you invent things?"

For the first time since he'd come into the police station, I saw him smile, faintly, briefly. "You follow the routine," he said. "And you hope for luck."

"Exactly. Now I wish you would go on home. I promise you'll be notified as soon as we know anything. And—there's always the possibility they might telephone you, or let her telephone you."

"And I need to answer. Not the answering machine." With surprising speed considering his earlier appearance of lethargy, he was up and heading for the door.

I dictated reports for an hour and then left for home.

I had left my car at a parking meter—with a quarter in the slot—about nine in the morning. It hadn't been towed, but it did have four parking tickets on it.

I had an undeposited check and no cash at all, because the robbery went down before I got to the banking window.

I drove over to Winn-Dixie, that big one they built a few years ago on Denton Highway, and bought a few groceries, writing a check that would certainly bounce if Harry or I didn't get to the bank first thing Monday morning, and went home.

· 3 ·

THEORETICALLY—ACCORDING TO THE books—a nine-week-old baby does not wake up for a two o'clock feeding. Cameron cannot yet read, and even if he could, I suspect he would be unwilling to allow a book to tell him whether he was hungry. He also does not believe in daylight saving time. I don't believe in it either, but I'm stuck with it just the same. All the howling in the world on my part will not change the clock.

All of which meant that at three in the morning by the clock—two by normal time—Cameron was awake and howling, without the slightest regard for the convenience of anybody else.

It is my firm opinion that if it can possibly be avoided no baby should be put on a bottle until he is through with 2 A.M. feedings. I mean, given the choice, why would any woman in her right mind want to get up and stagger around the kitchen warming a bottle, while the baby wakes up everybody in the house, when all she has to do is get up, change the baby, and crawl back into bed?

So I got up, changed the baby, and crawled back into bed, and Cameron had just quieted down when the telephone rang.

At 3 A.M.? That was unusual even for a cop's house. In my experience people who have not killed each other by 2 A.M. will generally wait until five or five-thirty to do it. I remember one horrible week when I was in ident that I got three call-outs in six nights, each one within five minutes one way or the other of 2 A.M. The third time, I opened one eye and looked at the clock and then I picked up the telephone receiver and said, "Where's the corpse?" Harry said I would have been very embarrassed if the caller hadn't been the dispatcher, but I still maintain that if the caller had been anybody else he'd have deserved the shock for calling people at that time of night.

But a totally unsurprised voice had replied, "Laying in the middle of Berry Street."

I couldn't recall ever getting a call between 2:15 and 5:30 A.M. To a homicide or anything else.

But all the same the telephone was shrilling into the night, and I tried—with limited success—to answer it without detaching Cameron, who prefers not to be disturbed when he is feeding.

"Deb?" said a voice I recognized as Darla Hendricks, a fairly new dispatcher I'd previously known as a clerk-typist in records. "I'm afraid we've found Dorene Coe."

"Oh, shit," I said. The apologetic tone left no doubt as to the condition in which Dorene Coe had been found. "Where?"

"Trinity Park. A patrol car found her. Shot in the head."

"Execution-style?" I asked. Even amateurs do that now. They've learned it from the movies.

"Looked like it. How soon can you get there?"

"An hour."

"An *hour?*"

"An hour," I said firmly. It would take me approximately twenty-five minutes to throw on my clothes and drive over to Trinity Park in the middle of the night with almost no traffic on the road. It would take approximately another half hour to finish feeding Cameron.

"Okay," Darla said. "I'll let Millner know." Her voice reflected my own expectations as to Millner's acceptance of that proposed schedule.

It took exactly seven minutes for the telephone to ring again. Captain Millner's voice sounded wrathful. "What do you mean, you can't get over here for an hour?"

"I'm feeding the baby," I said.

"Let Harry feed the baby."

"Harry," I said with as much dignity as I could muster, "doesn't have the equipment."

"Oh, hell," Millner said. "Deb, you ever hear of a bottle?"

"He won't *take* a bottle."

We compromised. I fed Cameron for ten more minutes, by which time he was full enough that he'd consent to think about a bottle, and Harry got up to make the bottle while I dressed and took off for Trinity Park.

In the daytime, this is a very nice place to be. The children's railroad from Forest Park Zoo runs over here. There are picnic tables, and ponds with ducks, and playground equipment. This is where they hold the Mayfest; this is where they hold Shakespeare in the Park. There are stepping-stones so that you can walk across the Trinity River to the office buildings and restaurants on the other side, or, if you are in a mood such that you demand to be completely let alone, you can walk out on the stepping-stones and sit down on the largest one, right in the middle of the river, and let the river flow past you on either side, as I have done a few times. I don't know what they do about the stepping-stones during the Mayfest; I would think they would get in the way of the inner-tube races, but maybe they are considered some sort of an obstacle course.

In the daytime. In the daytime.

I wouldn't want to go to Trinity Park at night unless there were a lot of other people there too, as there are during Shakespeare in the Park or the Mayfest.

Dorene Coe presumably hadn't wanted to go to Trinity Park at night either.

She was lying on the grass near the stepping-stones, still in the green silk dress; the bright paisley scarf, only slightly disarranged, was clearly visible in the patrol car spotlight that was turned on her. She was still wearing the gold neck chain, the gold Seiko watch, the multicolored strapped sandals. Even her hair wasn't disarranged much. She was lying on her stomach, face turned to the left. She'd been shot once behind the left ear; the entry wound looked bigger than a .38, which said the exit wound on the right, when we turned her over, wasn't going to be pretty.

I had no doubt whatever that she'd done exactly what they told her to do. She'd done exactly as she was told and they'd killed her for it. I don't usually cry at crime scenes but tears were running down my face, for Dorene Coe's stolen life, for Robert Coe's grief, for that memory I knew I would never, never, never be able to forget, the memory of Dorene Coe's face as she looked at me, as she walked out the door of the bank to be killed.

Her car wasn't there. The blue Lynx wasn't there. There weren't even any tire tracks, but why should there be any tire tracks? There is a nice little asphalt road that goes all through the park, and I could see no reason why the car—whichever car they used—would ever have had to get off the asphalt. Dorene had, almost certainly, walked from wherever the car was stopped to the place she was killed. There was no physical evidence; there was nothing, nothing, nothing at all to go on. I wasn't crying now; grief had been replaced by anger, by complete rage. There was no reason to kill Dorene Coe. No reason at all.

And I didn't want to catch these robbers-turned-killers just because I was a police officer, not anymore. I wanted to catch them because of that utter rage I was feeling.

The rage we—I—would never be able to communicate to a judge or a jury, because in court all that can come out is facts. Just the facts, ma'am. Anything else is considered prejudicial.

I stepped to the side, watching the lab crew set to work, and I remembered a discussion I'd had twenty years ago with an acquaintance who disapproved not only of execution, but also of imprisoning criminals. When I asked what she thought *should* be done about criminals she had no answers, but she was sure the entire judicial system as it presently exists is totally wrong. "But, Trish," I said, "suppose that somebody kidnapped, raped, and murdered one of your daughters, what would you think should be done about that criminal?"

"That's not the point," she said to me. "You're inserting a personal element now."

"That's exactly the point," I told her. "Every crime is personal to its victims, to their families."

We had to agree to disagree. I couldn't understand her and she couldn't understand me. But standing under the trees watching Irene Loukas photograph this corpse, I wished everyone who believed what Trish believed could be required to ride with a big-city homicide unit for one week.

Not, of course, that that would do any good. Very few people allow their heartfelt beliefs to be altered by anything so insignificant as a fact or two.

A patrolman stood between me and the corpse, elbows bent and hands resting on his hips, and I was looking through the crook of his elbow over his gun butt at the body. *I'd like to have a picture of this*, I thought. *A picture of the dead woman lying on the grass with the patrolman standing as he was standing, a picture I could show to people as the definitive answer when they ask what a cop's life is really like. It's like this, I could reply. It's senseless, meaningless death of people who shouldn't have died, at least not where and when and how they died. It's the disgust and rage and futility that all cops feel at this senseless, mindless waste of human life, of human potential. I wish you could see it like this.*

The ambulance had arrived before I had, and the driver and his helper were waiting patiently to be told they could transport the body. Now another car arrived, a beige station wagon belonging to the medical examiner's office. Deputy medical examiner Andrew Habib and medical examiner's investigator Gil Sanchez got out, and Gil at once began taking the same photo series Irene Loukas had just taken. I always wonder why they don't just share photos, instead of duplicating each other's work, but mine not to reason why.

While Gil was taking pictures Habib stood beside me. "What've you got?" he asked me.

I told him.

"*Coe?*" he asked unbelievingly. "*Dorene* Coe? *Robert* Coe's—?"

Several times we've had corpses I had known as people. Now, I surmised, we finally had a corpse that Habib had known as a person.

"Coe," I agreed. "Dorene Coe. Robert Coe's wife."

"Damn," Habib said. "What son of a bitch would want to kill that little girl?"

"A scared son of a bitch," I replied. "A son of a bitch she could identify." Habib nodded.

Sanchez finished taking his pictures, and Habib and I went over to the body, which was now formally—if a little unnecessarily—ruled a body. Formally, because the law requires an official pronouncement of death. Unnecessarily, because the body had cooled considerably and postmortem lividity—that staining that shows the position the body was lying in—was advanced.

Habib, for once not humming at a crime scene, checked her wrist for rigor mortis (there wasn't any), looked at the lividity, looked at his watch, made some rapid calculations, and said, "Ten o'clock. Give or take a little."

This time of year, with daylight saving time, it wasn't going to be full dark much before ten o'clock. There should have still been people in the park—joggers, lovers. Somebody should have heard a shot. Should, maybe, have seen the car, maybe even have seen the killer.

But nobody had reported a shot. Nobody had reported a body.

Nobody saw it? Or nobody wanted to get involved?

The ambulance attendants came and turned the body over, for Gil and Irene to photograph the exit wound.

You are allowed to photograph only the wound. You can't introduce into court anything likely to inflame the jury.

But the camera, catching the dirty, bloody, torn exit wound, incredibly huge compared to the entry wound, couldn't avoid also catching the half-open eyes and the delicate childlike curve of the cheek and jaw.

I wasn't thinking like a cop tonight. I tried to excuse myself on the grounds that I'd been away from the job for almost three months, but that wasn't the reason at all. The real reason was—

Was no use thinking about.

The ambulance crew removed the body.

Irene photographed the spray of blood, skin, skull fragments, and brain tissue lying on the spring-green grass surrounding the small hole the slug had drilled in the ground. Then, wearing plastic gloves, she began to dig for the slug, carefully so as not to scratch it when she found it.

It hadn't gone deep. Earth stops slugs more efficiently than brain tissue does. Irene slipped it into a plastic evidence bag, wrote the case number, date, time, place, and her initials on the evidence tag, and handed it to me. I added my initials before examining it closely in the glare of the spotlights.

To my admittedly inexpert eyes, it looked like a .357 Magnum.

Dorene Coe, alive, probably hadn't weighed ninety-five pounds.

"There's no use trying to do anything else," I heard Irene saying to Millner. "It's too blinkin' dark. In the morning—"

"I'll have somebody sit on it till morning," Millner agreed. He radioed for a squad car, somebody who could be left to protect the crime scene; after some discussion with dispatch, it was agreed that two cars would be necessary even if that did leave fewer cars on the road than was optimal.

I went to the police station, locked the slug in an evidence locker, and began to dictate a report onto a tape recorder. Captain Millner wandered in around 5 A.M. and said, "Why don't you take Sunday off?"

That didn't deserve an answer. I just glared at him.

"I mean it," he said. "The FBI is on it too—"

I turned off the tape recorder and hit REWIND, STOP, PLAY to get back to where I was before the interruption. "I'm not scheduled to work Sunday," I pointed out.

"So take off—"

"*I'm already here,*" I yelled.

"What?"

"It *is* Sunday," I said more calmly, "and I'm here. How can I not do what I've already done?"

"You can go home," he said, "and try to teach that kid of yours to drink a bottle."

At that point I disgraced myself utterly. I burst into tears.

By the time I got through crying Captain Millner had left, which was probably very smart of Captain Millner, and I decided to go home too, stopping at the Stop and Go on the corner near my house to buy more milk for breakfast, Hal having consumed most of a gallon of milk during supper. The morning *Star-Telegram* was already on the rack at Stop and Go. The headlines informed me that Robert Coe had offered a sizable reward, no questions asked, for the safe return of his wife. That nearly set me off again.

I drove the remaining four blocks home and managed to get in the door approximately two minutes before Cameron decided it was breakfast time. So I changed the baby and took him to bed with me, waking abruptly three hours later with the realization that Cameron, the bed, and I were all going to have to be changed and washed most thoroughly. You would think by now, with three other children, I would remember the kind of things that happen when you go to sleep with a baby in bed with you. But on the other hand I'd had sixteen years to forget.

By the time that chore was finished and the washer was running with the first of the two loads that were going to be necessary, I had missed church. Well, to be honest, I hadn't really exactly missed church. This church that Hal has joined, and I attend sporadically, makes very efficient use of its space; three congregations, called wards, all meet in the same building and of course they stagger their times. This year our ward had sacrament meeting starting at one in the afternoon, with Sunday school and the other assorted meetings after it. So I still had plenty of time to get to church, except that I had made up my mind I wasn't going to go. By now I was back into a nightgown, and unless I had to, I wasn't going anywhere else today that required me to put my clothes on.

Rather sleepily I told Hal he'd have to get a ride to church—that was no problem; he could ride with any of five families that lived within a one-mile radius of us—and I put Cameron in the playpen to eat his Cradle Gym. That also was no problem; Cameron will put anything in his mouth except a baby bottle. And I went into the kitchen and began to read cookbooks.

I am a little vague as to why I read cookbooks on Saturday and Sunday mornings, because I know perfectly well that sooner or later I am going to make muffins. But I always read cookbooks in case the inspiration to do something else strikes me.

As usual, it did not, and by ten-fifteen—which is a little late for breakfast but fairly typical for me on a weekend morning—I had put the muffins in the oven. Harry for once was not talking on the ham radio; he was reading something he tried, not very successfully, to hide from me as I went back into the living room.

Of course I asked what it was. Wouldn't you?

Reluctantly he produced it. It was a large, glossy brochure from something called the Napoleon Hill Institute of Management, which said, in small letters on the back page, that it was named for Napoleon Hill but was in no way affiliated with him. "I was thinking about getting an MBA," he said.

"An MBA?" I repeated.

"Deb, I can't fly anymore," he said, and that was the first time he'd been able to say that without his voice breaking. "I can't fly anymore. I've been a helicopter pilot nearly thirty years, but I'm through. I can't fly a helicopter anymore. And the problem is I can't do anything else. I've got a lot in my brain. The company'd still have a use for me, if I could go into management."

"They can't promote you into management without a degree in management?"

"They can," he said. "Deb, I didn't tell you, but they offered me a promotion. The trouble is—the trouble is I can't do the job. Not now. I just don't know how. I read some of the stuff they wanted me to do and I didn't understand it. But if I got a degree in management—"

"But from a fly-by-night school—"

"It isn't fly-by-night," he said, a little crossly.

"I mean, couldn't you go to TCU, or Arlington, or—"

"I don't know if I could get in to one of them, or if I could do the work if I did. It's been nearly thirty years since I've been in college. You know that. I don't know if I could do the work. But this place, it's geared to people like me. I checked, Deb. It's accredited. And I checked with

Bell. They'll pay my tuition as long as I maintain a B average. It's night school. One night a week. I can—I can stay home with the baby in the daytime. And maybe, maybe after I get the degree and go back to work, maybe then you can quit and stay home. I know you want to."

I didn't say I wanted to stay home now, not two years from now. He already knew that.

And he'd been locked in gloom and depression ever since the accident, alternating between insisting the doctor was wrong and he would be able to fly again, and sitting on the couch staring into space. I was glad he wasn't a drinking man, because I was sure he'd have been drinking if he were. This was the first positive sign I'd seen.

"It sounds like a good idea," I said. "When will you start?"

"I haven't decided to," he said. "I'm just thinking about it."

"Oh. If you don't do that, then what—"

"I don't know," he said, sounding ready to cry again.

I decided to go see what I could think of to go with the muffins. Like maybe a ham and cheese omelet. This was no time to be worrying about cholesterol.

The noon news reported the murder, and a little before one o'clock Detective Nathan Drucker, who'd lately been assigned to join us in the major case squad, called me. "I've got a couple of kids down here who think they might have seen the killing," he said. "You want me to get statements from them, or you want to come on in?"

Cameron was going to have to agree to a bottle at two o'clock, or else he'd have to wait until I got home, I decided, dressing rapidly and heading out the door. After all, who's the boss, me or a nine-week-old baby?

Anybody who's ever had a nine-week-old baby—and many people who haven't—knows the answer to that. The baby, of course. When Cameron howls he howls loudly. Pat, the half-Doberman half-pit bull who is the reason we have a six-foot chain-link fence all around the yard (free dogs can be *very* expensive), comes to the back door and whines when Cameron howls. The cat, which I am someday going to give to my son-in-law (the future psychiatrist son-in-law, not the lawyer son-in-law), goes and sits on the dresser with its tail wrapped around all four legs and looks down very curiously at the crib below. Sometimes the cat gets in the crib and purrs loudly. This does not discourage Cameron from howling unless he's howling because he's bored, not because he is hungry, in which case he tries to grab the cat's tail, which he apparently considers some sort of handle. Eventually this results in renewed howling, because the cat prefers not to let its handle be grabbed. But the thought of getting out of the crib never crosses whatever excuse for a mind the cat has. No, the cat remains in the crib, twitching its tail just enough to keep it out of reach of Cameron's hand.

On second thought maybe I had better not give the cat to Olead and Becky, my younger daughter and her husband. Cameron's older-than-he-is nephew—my older daughter Vicky's son Barry—is to be joined, in about seven months, by a niece or nephew younger than he is. In other words, Becky is now gestating. As she already has Olead's three-year-old half brother, now her and Olead's adopted son, to chase, she doesn't need a cat who teases babies to add to the commotion.

With that rather grumpy thought, I parked in a vacant lot beside the police station and went in.

Mike Howell and Janelle Parker both seemed about the age of my older son, sixteen or so. They both looked like nice, normal, well-dressed, well-brought-up middle-class kids. Mike was white and Janelle was black and the main thing they seemed concerned about was making sure their parents didn't find out they were together last night. Neither set approved.

"I certainly won't go and tell them," I said, "and I expect we can keep it from the press for now. But if it goes to trial—"

"Um," Mike said, and looked at Janelle.

Janelle shrugged. "We'll testify if we have to," she said.

"But my mama, she'll really get mad if she finds out about Mike."

"And my dad—" Mike said, and shook his head. "Right now I'm supposed to be out shooting baskets with Orrin, and Janelle's supposed to be at choir practice."

"Where were you supposed to be last night?" I asked.

"I was spending the night with my sister," Janelle said. "She'll cover for me."

"And my dad knows I was on a date," Mike said. "He just doesn't know who with."

"And you think you might have seen the killing?"

They both nodded.

"Tell me about it."

"We were—um—at the park," Mike said. "I was borrowing my mom's car. We were—we weren't doing anything, you know, we shouldn't be doing."

"We were feeding the ducks," Janelle said softly. "I had some stale bread and we were feeding the ducks in the pond. And this car drove past us kind of fast."

"A white New Yorker," Mike said. "And you know how curvy the roads in the park are. It was going too fast. That was why I looked at it. That, and just the car. It was real—" He stopped, fumbling for words. "Yuppie. It was a real yuppie kind of car."

"Could you see who was in it?"

"Yeah. There was—were four people in it. A guy and a girl in the front, and a guy and a girl in the back."

"Can you describe them?"

"Not from then, but they got out of the car. They got out of the car at the duck pond and then they got back in and drove off again, still too fast. They drove toward the river, and we got through feeding the ducks and we were walking around, you know, just walking around not really going anywhere, just walking, and we saw the car had stopped and they had got out of it again. The one guy, I think he was the one driving, was tall, about six-two, six-three, something like that, and the other guy was a lot shorter, maybe about five-six. They both had dark-brown hair, or maybe it was almost black, it was hard to tell because it was getting dark. The one lady had blond hair and the other lady's hair was kind of brownish. Light brown, light enough I could tell it was brown and not blond or black even in that light."

"How were they dressed?"

"Both guys and the blond lady had on jeans and both men had on T-shirts," Mike said. "The other lady—" He looked at Janelle.

"She had on a green dress," Janelle said. "It was—elegant. The kind of thing, you can look at it and you're pretty sure she didn't buy it at K mart. Maybe Dillards. Most likely Neiman-Marcus. But real simple. Real, real simple. The blond lady, she had on this candy-striped blouse. It was K mart. Or maybe Wal-Mart."

"You said the men had on T-shirts. What—"

Janelle and Mike looked at each other. "Just T-shirts," Janelle said. "I couldn't tell any more. Or maybe I could, but I don't remember now. Just T-shirts. Light colored. They might have had some sort of writing on them but I don't remember. The taller guy had on a baseball cap but I couldn't tell what color or if it had anything written on it."

"What makes you think they were the killers?" I asked.

"In the newspaper this morning it said what the lady was wearing," Janelle said. "And then on the TV at noon it said she—it said she got killed. Right there in the park."

"And we—I think we were there," Mike said. "Right there. They were—we heard this *pop*. Just before we came over the hill. We had seen the car pass us but we didn't know it had stopped again and we heard this kind of a pop noise like a loud firecracker—"

"More like a cherry bomb," Janelle interrupted. "Too loud for a regular firecracker."

"More like a cherry bomb," Mike agreed. "And then we went over the hill and then we saw them and the blond lady was lying on the ground but I didn't think nothing about it because people are always lying down in the park.

I just—" He swallowed. "I just said, 'Hey, mister, it's against the law to pop firecrackers here,' and the tall guy, he said, 'Oh, is it? Then we won't pop any more.' And he sat down on the ground and Janelle and I went on."

"And you didn't walk back that way?"

"Uh-uh," Janelle said. "We'd left the car in the parking lot on the other side of the dike, and we went back the other way. I just keep thinking, if we'd walked back that way we would have found her."

"And if we'd found her and they knew it—" Mike said, and didn't finish. He looked at me. "I thought it was firecrackers," he said. "I just thought it was firecrackers."

I got a written statement, trying unsuccessfully to figure out how many times the car had stopped, and sent them home, knowing as I watched them leave that these two children had just left childhood behind. They had gone to the park to feed the ducks and maybe pet a little, and they had seen murder. Nothing was ever going to change that.

But for Dorene Coe, only four years older, it wasn't just childhood that was over. It was life.

I dictated a supplemental report and was just getting ready to go home when the receptionist—we now have one even on Sunday—rang my desk. "Ed Gough is here," she said.

That is pronounced "Goff." I knew Ed Gough. Every cop in town knows Ed Gough. "Send him in," I said resignedly, wondering how long it would take me to get rid of him this time.

He came in, in khaki pants that were too short for him and a khaki shirt that was too large. He had a baseball cap on his head, crammed on so awkwardly that his graying brown hair stuck out in all directions. He took the cap off as he sat down at my desk and leaned forward confidentially. "I did it, you know," he said.

"Fine, Ed, can we talk about it tomorrow?" I asked hopelessly.

"No, I got to tell you now," he said.

A long time ago—twenty-five years ago—Ed Gough really did do it. He raped and strangled his sister, in a downtown park on a Sunday afternoon, and the courts ruled him insane at the time of the strangling and insane at the time of the trial, and they put him away for a long time. But finally, about seven years ago, the doctors decided he was sane enough to turn loose, and turn him loose they did. Ever since then Ed Gough comes in to confess to murder after murder after murder, two or three times a month. And you always have to listen, because there is always the possibility that this time he might be telling the truth.

This time I didn't think he was. But he was the right size—six-two—and he was the right race and he was the right sex and he had killed before. I had to listen.

"Then tell me," I said.

"She had on a green dress."

This might have seemed evidentiary, except that—again as every cop in Fort Worth knew by now—Ed Gough's sister had been wearing a green dress.

"Uh-huh," I said. "What else?"

"I killed her," he said.

"Uh-huh," I said. "How did you kill her?"

"I didn't mean to."

"Okay."

"I wanted to stop her screaming. She was screaming and screaming and screaming and I wanted her to stop. So I put my hands over her mouth and she bit me and she went on screaming and so I had to make her stop screaming and so I put my hands on her throat so the screams couldn't get out and I squeezed and squeezed and squeezed—No?"

I was shaking my head. "No, Ed, not this time."

"That wasn't how I killed her?"

"You didn't kill this one, Ed," I told him. "That was somebody else, a long time ago. Not this one."

"But she had on a green dress," he said. "The television said she had on a green dress."

"It was a different green dress."

"Oh. So you aren't going to lock me up?"

"Not today."

"You really ought to lock me up," he said.

"Why's that?"

"So I won't kill somebody else," he said, and for a moment he sounded completely sane and very worried. He shook his head. "I know who I killed. I killed Debbie. That's who I killed. It was a long time ago. I didn't mean to kill her. I didn't want to kill her. But I couldn't stop. And they locked me up and they kept me locked up so I couldn't kill anybody else but then they turned me loose and I killed another one but nobody believes me."

"We can't find another one that you killed," I said.

"But I did. I really did."

"But not yesterday."

"No. Not yesterday. But I killed another one. And she had on a green dress just like Debbie did."

This was at least the fourth time he'd told me this story, the fourth time in the forty or fifty times he'd confessed to just about any killing on the books. My friend Susan Braun is a psychiatrist; I'd talked to her about it, and she'd said he probably did kill another woman.

But in the seven years Ed had been back on the streets we didn't have a woman reported missing who was supposed to have been wearing a green dress, and we didn't have a woman reported missing who fitted the description he'd given of the woman he said he killed.

"You've got to lock me up," he was saying urgently.

"Ed, I can't lock you up," I told him. "Maybe you did kill somebody else, but I can't find the body, and you didn't kill the woman yesterday."

"But I could have."

"Maybe you could have. But you didn't. Go on home now, and stay out of trouble."

Ed turned to look at Nathan. "Will *you* lock me up?"

Nathan shook his head. "I would if I could, Ed, but I can't."

"Somebody's got to lock me up," Ed muttered, and stalked out of the office, jamming the baseball cap back on his head.

"Someday he is going to kill somebody else," Nathan said, "and then the press is going to ask why the police couldn't prevent it."

"Or," I returned, "someday somebody's going to be razing a house or digging up a vacant lot and they're going to dig up a skeleton in a green dress." I closed my desk drawer. "I'm going home."

Home. Where, just like yesterday, my husband and my son were going to be sitting patiently waiting for me to come home and prepare supper.

In the past this problem has been solved by going out to a cafeteria or to the Red Lobster, but the arrival of Cameron had made that expedient a little less simple. Last night I jammed three frozen pizzas in the oven. Tonight I solved it by stopping by Kentucky Fried Chicken. The long-range solution might be to introduce Harry to a cookbook.

Cookbook, this is Harry.

Harry, this is a cookbook.

Harry, this is my kitchen.

Forget it.

Thank heaven for Kentucky Fried Chicken, carryout pizza and Chinese food, Red Lobster, cafeterias, and Shake 'n Bake.

And I really am going to have to figure out a way to get Cameron to take a bottle.

· 4 ·

HAL AND HIS GIRLFRIEND Lori were in the front yard teasing the dog, alternating between throwing a ball for him to chase and pretending to throw the ball. Pat, who is not the world's most intelligent canine, would go tearing off after the ball just as readily whether it was thrown or not, whereupon Hal would double up laughing until Lori got sorry for Pat and took the ball away from Hal to throw it out into the general direction where Pat was eagerly nosing around in the grass.

When I went in Hal and Lori—both in blue jeans, T-shirts, and dirty sneakers without laces (apparently shoelaces are déclassé this year)—followed me inside, Hal sauntering in that elaborately casual manner that usually means either he hopes not to be noticed (an impossible dream for someone who, at sixteen, is six foot five) or else he's getting ready to ask for something he doesn't expect to get. "Hi, stinker," he said amiably to Cameron, who was in the playpen eating his feet, which I think he is not yet supposed to be able to do.

"That's a *crummy* thing to call a baby!" Lori said indignantly.

"Then you change his pants next time," Hal said, "and you'll see why I call him stinker."

At this point we were joined by Pat, thoroughly proud of himself for having managed to get inside the house. For some incomprehensible-to-humans doggy reason, Pat adores Cameron. He stuck his nose up to the bars of the playpen and before anybody could grab him he had slurped an enormous kiss onto the baby, who did need his face washed but preferably not by a dog. Cameron looked immensely surprised but did not howl. "Hal, remove the dog and shut the door right this time," I said, going after a washcloth to rewash Cameron my way.

"Mom, can I borrow the pickup?" Hal asked, with one hand on Pat's collar. Without giving me time to answer, he went on hastily. "Because I have to change clothes and then I have to take Lori to change clothes because there's a youth fireside at church at seven."

"A *fireside?*" I demanded. "In *this* weather?" May, in Tarrant County, is not full summer, but it doesn't miss it far, and the thermometer had not been under ninety degrees in daylight for two weeks.

"Not a *real* fireside," Hal explained. "It's just called a fireside. It's really this sort of meeting where we have a meeting and stuff like that, and we'll be home, I mean I'll be home about nine or maybe nine-thirty, so can I use the pickup?"

"It's your father's pickup," I said. "Ask him."

"He says I have to ask you because of the defishalation."

"Because of the *what?*"

"The budgetary defishalation. Or something like that. Because we can't afford much gasoline because Dad's out of work."

"The budgetary deficit?"

"Maybe that was it."

"Yes, you may borrow the pickup truck if it's okay with your dad," I said. "I rarely if ever forbid you to go to church."

"Thanks, Mom." Leaving Lori to remove a very large half Doberman, half pit bull from the house—to put this in proportion, you should be aware that Lori is approximately five foot four and the average pit bull can tow a pickup truck—Hal tore off to change clothes. That is, he put a clean T-shirt on. That seemed to be all the changing he was doing. Then he and Lori left while I fed Cameron and put him down to nap until he decided it was time to eat again.

I then went to change clothes myself, hoping I wasn't going out again tonight, and Harry followed me into the bedroom. "Hal," he pointed out, "is gone for the evening."

"That's true," I agreed.

"And Cameron seems to be asleep."

"That also is true."

"Well," Harry said, and added, "I took the phone off the hook."

That was the best idea I had heard in simply weeks.

Monday morning, and I was officially back at work. As I had already logged eight hours over the weekend, I could have declared myself to be taking comp time and stayed home. That would have salved my conscience in relation to Cameron for one more day, but of course it would have done nothing at all for my conscience in relation to Dorene Coe.

So I got up at six (I had no choice on that), fed Cameron, fed myself (Harry is good about making breakfast), and took off to work, leaving Harry to cope with Cameron at ten o'clock and two o'clock. There was plenty of formula. There were plenty of bottles. I fully anticipated that the bottles would be full, and Cameron would be empty and howling, when I got home. How do you persuade a kid to take a bottle?

There was no such problem with my other children. I adopted them, and in fact every one of them was past Cameron's present age before I acquired them. They were already on bottles.

You would think, after making reports all weekend, I would have no more reports to make. That is a joke. Police departments float on a sea of paperwork. I had officially been back at work for five minutes and already I was three reports behind. Also I had a full—a very, very full—in basket, most of its contents consisting of things that I, or somebody, should have done one, two, or three months ago. I went through it fast, consigning most of it to the trash except for the stuff that had to be read, initialed, and passed on, which I initialed without reading and sneaked into Nathan's in basket while he wasn't looking.

I was still coping with the in basket when Dub Arnold and Donald Chang came in. I would like FBI agents a lot better if they dithered a lot less. As FBI agents go, Dub is fairly undithery—he's been around long enough to know that dithering doesn't help—but Donald Chang was another matter. He was just out of FBI agent school. He expected everything to be done right—J. Edgar Hoover style right, even if Hoover has been dead fifteen or so years—and he expected everything to be done right, right now. In the real world things do not work that way. He'd learn. But he didn't have to learn on my time.

Like it or not, however, this case was joint jurisdiction. The Fort Worth Police Department had jurisdiction because the robbery occurred in the city of Fort Worth, as did the murder. The FBI had jurisdiction because the FBI has jurisdiction on all bank robberies, whether or not they wind up in murders. I was the FWPD representative and Dub and Chang were the FBI representatives. That meant we had to work together.

Dub wanted us to go through the case file and then go

out and talk to witnesses. "There are two of you," I pointed out.

"So what?" Dub said, lounging comfortably in Dutch Van Flagg's chair. As Dutch's desk and mine face each other, that put him directly across from me.

"So if there are two of you what do you need me for?"

"Interagency cooperation," Dub drawled, and I said, "Shit!"

Donald Chang looked shocked. At the word, or at the fact that I was the one who said it, or at the lèse-majesté of a mere city detective being rude to an FBI agent?

"Dub, *look* at my desk," I protested. "I've been gone for three months. Can't you give me a couple of hours to catch my breath?"

"Deb, I'm sorry," Dub said. "We've got to go through the case file. You've got part of it and I've got part of it and nobody's got all of it, and you did some more after I left Saturday and you were back up here Sunday doing something. I've got to know what's going on. So either go through it with me or hand it over."

Of course he was right, and I was being a horse's rear end. "Let me check on something first," I said, and called the crime lab.

Irene—I sometimes wonder when Irene sleeps, as she seems to be present at all times whether or not she is scheduled to be on duty—answered, and I asked if they had finished the crime scene at the park. "Yeah, bright and early this morning," she assured me.

"I've got the FBI here. You got a report yet?"

"Tell the Flea-Bitten Idiots they can damn well wait," she replied. "I'll have it when I have it."

"How soon is that?"

"Who needs it? Them or you?"

"Both of us," I said.

"Give me half an hour."

I relayed that information—without the side remarks—

and Dub nodded. "If I'd asked for it it would have taken two days," he commented.

"Why's that?" Chang asked.

"It's a long, long story," Dub told him. "Let me put it this way. When you—that's you you, not a generic you—think of crime scene work you think of our own lab. But the fact is our lab is over a thousand miles away and usually three months backed up. When we need lab work done fast we ask the local police department." Ignoring Chang's look of disapproval, he went on. "That's just the way it is. It's the way it has been for a long time. We scratch their backs and they scratch our backs. But once upon a time, Chang, there was a young fella assigned to me for training, just like you, who didn't understand that when people are doing us a favor we act nice to those people. He got real, real, real pissed off at Irene Loukas for getting a report to us three days late, without stopping to think that Irene Loukas didn't owe us a report—or a crime scene—at all. And Irene Loukas got real, real, real pissed off at us as a result. And she stayed that way. Let that be a lesson to you," he said pontifically. "Don't bite the hand that—uh—scratches your back."

I had to laugh at that. I remembered Irene on the witness stand one time—this was in a burglary trial—when the defense attorney, who was about the same age and had about the same degree of experience as Donald Chang, asked her whether she was sure of the fingerprint identification she had made. She said she was sure, and the attorney asked her whether she had asked the FBI to confirm the identification. Now, that was a very silly question—a fingerprint expert is a fingerprint expert, no matter what department the expert works for—and Irene replied, "No, sir, I did not."

"And why didn't you?"

"That's not standard procedure."

Very stupidly, the attorney kept probing, until finally he had Irene—he thought—boxed into a corner. That was when Irene replied, "Sir, you don't seem to understand what I'm saying. I don't ask the FBI for help. The FBI asks me for help."

The defense attorney's gasp was audible, and the district attorney, insisting with injured innocence that his witness had been unjustly impugned, took over long enough to elicit from Irene a list of ten times the FBI had asked her for assistance.

Why am I telling this story now? Because it might—might—be applicable. We didn't—so far—have any fingerprints from any of the suspects. In the past that wouldn't really have made any difference; the FBI couldn't run latent checks because they might take years to do. Now, with the new computerized fingerprint system, a latent check—comparing a single fingerprint from a crime to the massive FBI fingerprint files—is possible, and in the case of bank robberies they are likely to be faster because the FBI maintains a separate file of bank robber fingerprint cards. But there are millions upon millions of fingerprint cards in the FBI files and even with computers, checking them all could take weeks or even months.

But that didn't matter, because we had no fingerprints. What we had, from the rearview mirror, was a chunk of palm print. The FBI says that making nonsuspect idents from palm prints is impossible.

Irene did it once. Only once, but that was enough to prove it was not impossible. It wasn't going to be fast, but if the palm print of "Melanie Griffith" was on file sooner or later Irene was going to identify it. Although our fingerprint file is large, our palm print file is small, but without a classification system—a few classification systems for palm prints have been devised but none of them are really practical, the way the Henry or the Vucetich or the FBI systems are for fingerprints—it was going to take a very long time to manually search that small fragment of palm print against every palm print we had on file. Not only the women, but also the men, just in case it had been one of the male suspects, rather than the female, who had left that chunk of print.

I knew without having to ask her that she'd already done the obvious things; she'd checked the name "Melanie Griffith" and she'd checked anything similar, like "Griffen" and "Griffin," to see if any of them checked out. She'd have told me if they had.

So we had one lead that we could check that the FBI couldn't—or at least wouldn't—check. I didn't have to spell it out for Dub, except to see to it he read the report mentioning the piece of palm print, because he knew Irene. I wasn't going to bother to spell it out for Chang. Let Dub tell him, if he needed to be told.

I handed Dub my case file, such as it was—some of the reports from Saturday and Sunday hadn't been typed yet—and went on fiddling with my in basket. After a while Irene called me to say that her report was on the computer if I wanted a printout. I got a printout and handed it to Dub and returned to the in basket again. "Deb?" Dub said.

"Yeah?" I did not look up. Almost to the bottom of the in basket, I still was not at all disposed to rejoin the world.

"It looks to me like if we're going to find anything it's going to be in the victim's car."

"I agree. If we could find the victim's car."

Dub was rustling papers. "White New Yorker, practically brand new. Ought to be easy to find."

"Ought to be," I agreed, "but it hasn't turned up yet."

"Chang, go down and get me a Coke," Dub said. After Chang was out of earshot, he said, "You don't want to talk with me."

"Nothing personal. I don't want to talk with anybody."

"If I'd been in your shoes I'd have done the same thing. Said the same thing."

I didn't answer. I didn't want to answer.

"So you gave good advice and the situation went sour. That's never happened to anybody else in the whole entire history of the world."

"Knock it off, Dub," I said.

"Damned if I'll knock it off. You listen to me—"

"Dub, will you just shut up?" I screamed. "That woman—that nineteen-year-old girl—is *dead!*"

"Yes, she's dead. But you didn't do it. It happens. It happens, that's all. Yes, a nineteen-year-old girl died, and yes, it was a cruddy thing to happen. Yes, she looked at you on her way out the door, and yes, maybe she blamed you. That doesn't mean you did anything wrong. What would have happened if you *hadn't* said what you did? There might have been ten people dead instead of one."

"*Might-have-been*'s ass," I retorted. "I have to live with what *did* happen."

"That's right," Dub said. "So you do. And so does every man who's ever been in a command position and given orders in combat. Sometimes people get killed. Sometimes—usually—the wrong people get killed. There's nothing you can do about it. You have to live with it. Yes. You do have to live with it. So crawl out of that damned stack of papers and face the world. Quit feeling sorry for yourself and let's get out and clear this case."

"You got any brilliant wonderful suggestions on just how we're going to go about accomplishing that miracle? Dub, we haven't got anything to go on except one chunk of palm print, and Irene's doing her best on it but I don't have to tell you how long that's going to take to do any good, if it ever does."

"Let's you and me go out and talk with Coe and see if we can get any more description on that white New Yorker. Anything that might help us to distinguish it from any other white New Yorker on the road."

"You and me, right," I said. "What about your tail?" Usually I am not that rude on the subject of rookies. After all, we were all rookies once. But today I just felt mean. And there was something indefinable about Donald Chang that reminded me of Dan Quayle.

Donald Chang, who had wandered back in sometime in the last few seconds with a paper cup of Coca-Cola, looked offended at my calling him a tail. "He goes too," Dub said. He took the cup, drained it, dropped it into a trash can, and said, "Let's go. Grab a walkie-talkie."

Surprise, surprise. We even used the FBI's car. This rarely happens. Catch the feds spending their own money when they can spend the city's. I've even found them making long-distance calls on our phones instead of using their own nice government WATS lines. I suspect we were using Dub's car this time only because Dub was perfectly aware that Robert Coe was fairly near the top of the list of human beings I did not want to talk with today, and he wasn't at all sure we'd ever get there if we went in my car. I might think of one, or two, or two dozen detours and other errands we had to run on the way.

Robert Coe's house didn't look like the kind of place you'd expect a successful inventor to live. It was just a house, the kind a friend of mine once described as a plain vanilla house. It was brick because in this area almost all the houses are brick, and it had an enclosed garage because in this area almost all the houses have enclosed garages. It had, at a guess, three bedrooms, and it had a raggedy front yard of Bermuda grass already burned with the heat of May. It was really going to look bad by August.

I would have expected to find a lot of people there. There were no cars in front, and only a pickup truck about as dilapidated as Harry's in the driveway. "Are you sure this is the right house?" I asked uncertainly.

"It's the right house," Dub said, and knocked on the door.

Robert Coe came to the door in bare feet, khaki pants, and a T-shirt. His face looked drawn and the whites of his eyes were bloodshot. "What do you want?" he asked. "She's dead. There's nothing else you can do."

"We can try to find the killers," Dub said.

"What good will that do?"

"It might stop them from killing somebody else," Chang said. That was the correct response and, usually, the tactful one. Right now I suspected it was not tactful.

Coe's eyes shifted to me. "You're the one who told her to do what they said."

"Not just her. Everybody."

"Why did you do that?"

"To try to keep a shoot-out from getting started."

"So she was the only one who'd die."

"I hoped nobody would die," I said.

"She did do what they said. She did what they said and they shot her. What would have happened if she hadn't done what they said?"

"Nobody can answer that for sure," Dub said. "But most likely, they'd have shot her then and there and grabbed another hostage."

"What do you want now?" he asked again. "If there was anything I could have said that would help I'd have said it Saturday. I'd have gotten her back alive."

"Could we come in?" Dub asked. "Trying to stand here on the steps and talk—"

Coe shrugged and backed away from the door. "Come in."

The living room was as neat, as attractive, and as impersonal as a furniture store showroom; I surmised they must have done their real living in the den or the bedroom. Then, a few more steps inside the house, I saw the dining room to my right. The wooden table was big enough to seat twelve comfortably; that was all I could tell about it, because it was heaped, piled, with papers. Not newspapers, but every other kind of paper imaginable. Legal documents. Schematics. Letters. Clippings—one I noticed had the headline HIGH SCHOOL TEACHER/INVENTOR FIRED FOR MARRYING GIRL, 16.

Coe noticed the direction of my gaze. "Whatever you want, it's probably there," he said, and strode over to the table and began lifting things. "Patents—1980–1985. Patents—1986–1990. I have a lot of patents. My will. Dorene didn't have a will. She was only nineteen. What does a nineteen-year-old need a will for? I have a study. I have filing cabinets. I don't need to keep all this crap on the table. Dorene kept asking me to get it off the table and put it away so we could eat on the table instead of on TV trays and I kept saying I was going to. I was going to. I was going to. Whatever you're looking for, it's probably there."

"Mr. Coe, all we really want is a better description of her car," Dub said.

"Her car. What the hell difference does her car make? She's dead. She doesn't need a car. Dead women don't drive cars. I got her a nice car. I got her a New Yorker. Want the bill of sale? Here's the bill of sale. Here's the title. Here's the insurance—"

"Did it have any bumper stickers on it? Any—"

"Squirrel tails?" Coe finished bitterly. "No. It didn't have any bumper stickers. It didn't have any squirrel tails. She hated it. It was just like the living room. No personality. Dorene had a personality when we got married. But I swallowed her. I didn't mean to swallow her but I did. That was why she insisted on working—because at work she was Dorene, she wasn't Mrs. Robert Coe. I should have left her alone. I shouldn't have—"

"Can't some of your friends come over?" I asked. "You don't sound to me like you need—"

"To be alone? I'm always alone. I don't have any friends. I wouldn't let Dorene have any friends. I was always busy. I was too busy for friends. I was too busy for Dorene—" He began to weep, noisily.

And the walkie-talkie in my hand said, "Ten-three, ten thirty-three." Radio silence, major emergency. Automatically I touched the dial, to turn it up a little so Dub and Chang wouldn't have any trouble hearing it too.

There was an armed robbery in progress. The bank was two miles away.

Without even saying good-bye to Coe, the three of us turned and ran for the car.

· 5 ·

THE C&S BANK WAS so small, and so new, that it was still doing business out of a converted mobile home on Belknap while construction proceeded on the recently cleared lot behind the temporary building. By the time we arrived some three and a half minutes after getting the call, there were two patrol cars parked in front, and the construction workers had abandoned their framework and masonry to crowd around the trailer.

I could see one patrolman standing in front of the door. From this I deduced that the robber—or robbers—had been long gone before the first patrol car got here. Clearly I was right. Before Dub turned off the ignition the dispatcher was on the air: "All units, be on the lookout for beige Honda Accord, year unknown, being driven by Deandra Black, white female, five foot four, blond and blue. Subject is hostage. Vehicle will also be occupied by two male suspects. Suspect number one is white male, approximately six feet two, a hundred and sixty pounds, last seen wearing blue jeans and white T-shirt. Suspect number two is white male, approximately five foot seven, a hundred and forty pounds, last seen wearing blue jeans and yellow T-shirt. Suspects are armed with sawed-off shotguns."

Either it was a darn good copycat crime or it was the same two men—and I didn't think it was a copycat crime. What I did think was that Deandra Black was in bad trouble.

But clearly I wasn't to blame for this abduction, and maybe—just maybe—I wasn't as much to blame as I thought I was for the abduction and murder of Dorene Coe. Maybe they'd planned abductions to start with. Unless they'd gotten the idea from abducting Dorene Coe, and when it worked they'd decided to go on using it—

Oh, that was silly. There were no police cars in sight when they left with Deandra Black. This was their own idea.

Quite suddenly I had an idea. If it would work—if it would work—

I left the FBI agents to do whatever it was they wanted to do, while I grabbed a desk and a telephone book and started dialing.

A few minutes later, as I was on my sixth call, I became aware that Captain Millner was standing beside me looking more than a little bit annoyed. I glanced at him and kept on talking. "Right. If any of your people have let a car go out for a test drive—somebody who kept it out an hour or two, may not have it back yet—might have said they wanted to take it for a diagnostic check—right. I'm not in my office. I'm at—" I glanced at the telephone number and gave it. "But if they can't get through have them call the Fort Worth Police Department and they'll get in touch with me. Right. Thanks a lot."

I hung up. "Don't you think that could wait a few minutes, while we talk with witnesses?" Millner demanded, with barely concealed anger.

"No," I said. "Because last time they kept the car out several hours. They might do it again. If we can pick her up as she's returning the car, she can lead us to—"

"Um. Yeah." Millner took his glasses off and scratched the crease they had left on his nose. "See what you mean. Okay. Get on with it. Who all are you calling?"

For starters, I was calling every automobile dealer in northeast Tarrant County, because this bank was in northeast Tarrant County and I didn't think they had borrowed a car from the other side of town. For the robbery Saturday they got a car from University Chrysler-Plymouth; discounting that horrible intersection where I always get stuck, it was only about four miles from there to the place they'd pulled the robbery. If they'd kept that pattern they'd gotten this car from some place in the Birdville area—Richland Hills, North Richland Hills, Haltom City, something like that. They'd have gone a little farther afield than Saturday, maybe, because things are more spread out in this area than they are downtown, but they wouldn't have gone much farther.

If they'd kept that pattern.

If they'd kept that pattern.

Only do you know how many car dealerships—new and used—there are in the Birdville area? A lot more than you might think, if you haven't driven around there lately, or sat down with a telephone book or a city directory to try to figure out what was where.

But I was lucky. Sort of lucky.

Before I picked up the telephone again it rang. I answered it.

There wasn't anybody else there to answer it. Once again the robbers had struck while the branch manager was out of the building and the other teller was on break. Deandra had been the only teller there, and she was gone. The branch manager was back now, but he was outside talking with Donald Chang, and the teller who'd been on break was sitting in her car crying.

So, as I said, I answered the phone. "Detective Ralston?" asked an unfamiliar male voice.

"Yes, I'm Detective Ralston."

"My name is Harry Weaver, and I run Clean Harry's A-1 Used Cars?" He made it sound like a question.

"Yes, Mr. Weaver?"

"Well, um, you were trying to find somebody who'd taken a car on a test drive and hadn't come back?"

"Right." I wished he would sound less insecure. He was making me nervous.

"Yes, well, um, this lady came and took one out about an hour ago and she's not back yet. She left me her car."

"Is it a blue Lynx?"

"Uh-uh, no, it's this white New Yorker."

"White New Yorker," I repeated, feeling as if a bomb had just gone off in my midsection. "New?"

"Yeah, brand new. She told me she won it in one of those, like, magazine contests, and it was too big a car for her, and she was going to sell it and she was going to use part of the money she got for it to buy—"

"What car did she take out, Mr. Weaver?"

"Well, um—let me see, it's this white Chevrolet—" He gave me the year and the license plate number.

"What did she look like?"

"Oh, blond, I'd say about my wife's height—"

"How tall is that, Mr. Weaver?"

"Oh, I don't know, about five-seven—"

"Did she give you her name?"

"Yes, she said she was Carrie Fisher."

I did a double take at that one, and then my brain began to make connections. The kind of connections that Captain Millner usually refers to as jumping to conclusions. Because she—whoever she was—had used the name of Melanie Griffith to take a car out of University Chrysler-Plymouth. Now, Melanie Griffith could be a real name. In fact, Melanie Griffith *was* a real name—the name of the actress who starred opposite Harrison Ford in *Working*

Girl. And Carrie Fisher was the name of the actress who'd starred opposite Harrison Ford in three Star Wars movies.

Could I deduce I had a star-struck robbery accomplice?

Was I going to have to go and look up the names of every other actress who'd ever played opposite Harrison Ford to see what name this chick would be using next?

Maybe. And maybe not. Maybe I could lay hands on her before she became somebody else.

"Mr. Weaver, there will be police there shortly. Do your best not to let anybody near the New Yorker. If the woman comes back try to stall her if you can do it safely, but if she has a man with her just let her go. These people are very dangerous. Do you understand me?"

"Yes, I guess, but—"

"I'll talk to you later. Don't leave." I hung up fast and stood up fast and called dispatch to get a lookout on the Chevy. But after that I sort of went blank. There are times when the buck needs to be passed. "Captain Millner!" I said.

"In a minute," Millner said. He was talking with a witness.

"Now!" I yelled. "It can't wait."

Because the problem was, what did we do now? If we sent marked cars over to Clean Harry's, with lights and sirens, the chances were that they'd get there before she took the car back. But if she saw the lights and heard the sirens she probably wouldn't return the car at all. If I went over there quietly, by myself, with Dub and Chang because I wasn't in my own car right now, the chances were that she wouldn't notice anything wrong and would return the car, but the extra time would increase the likelihood that she would have already returned the Chevy and taken off before I got there.

If she intended to return the Chevy and retrieve the New Yorker at all, I thought belatedly. By now that New Yorker was mighty hot. It was, actually, surprising that she'd managed to drive it into a used car lot without a police car stopping her on the street.

I told Millner what was going on, and he looked around at Dutch Van Flagg, who had just entered the bank. "Take over here," he said. "I'm going with Deb. Hey, Dub, you hear me? I'm taking Deb with me."

"Uh-huh," Dub said, rather vaguely. He was in a lengthy colloquy with one of the workmen from the construction site. "Millner!" he called after us. "This guy says they got here in a white sedan, he thinks it's a Chevrolet. Some woman dropped them off and kept going."

"Right," Millner said. "We've got its plate number and broadcast a lookout already."

"How the hell did you do that?" Dub demanded. "You haven't even left the—"

"We're smart," Millner said. Grinning, he added, "Anyway, Deb's smart."

Chang looked at me. He looked very puzzled. That was okay with me; I didn't have to ride with him now. Millner and I left in a detective car.

Clean Harry's A-1 Used Cars—which, Millner pointed out, was a funny name for a used car lot—was on the 121 Frontage Road, which meant that you had to be going the right way to get to it and we weren't. That in turn meant that we had to pass it and double back on the freeway before we could even get onto the frontage road going the right way.

But when we finally did manage to get there, the white New Yorker was almost the first thing we saw. Coe was right; it didn't have any bumper stickers or squirrel tails. Dangling from the rearview mirror was the tag that said Dorene paid for monthly parking. That was the only thing on it that didn't come with the car, that and the license plates.

In it was another matter, of course. In it maybe—maybe—we would find something useful.

But that could wait. I wanted to talk with Weaver first.

He looked about as vague as he sounded. He was

maybe twenty-five, maybe thirty-five; he had the kind of looks that just don't change much. Sandy hair and blue eyes and a mildly receding chin that gave him a slightly rabbity look. It was easy to deduce—possibly incorrectly—that he sold used cars because he couldn't do anything else.

On the other hand he might well be a crackerjack used car salesman; that vague manner can be used to hide a very shrewd brain. I've known lawyers to pull that just-us-country-folks stunt and manipulate the juries wonderfully well. So was he a hick or a poker player? We'd know when we started talking with him.

Maybe.

Of course we radioed for ident. We'd get Bob Castle, because Irene was still at the bank robbery, but that was fine; Bob is a good ident tech too. Not that it would do much good, no matter what ident tech we had—these robbers didn't seem to leave their fingerprints lying around much.

I went through the same questions I'd asked at University Chrysler-Plymouth, and got about the same answers.

"She come here two or three times before," Weaver told me. "And it's kind of funny you should mention a blue Lynx. like you did over the phone, because always before when she come here she was in a blue Lynx. Said it had just got to where it wasn't hardly running, and she was gonna get another car. And then when she showed up in that big ol' New Yorker I said well, it looks like you did get you another car at that, and she kinda laughed and said well, she won this in one of them you-may-have-already-won contests and it was too big a car for her and she needed the money, so she was gonna sell it and get some money and just out an' out buy a used car. So I ast her if she was still gonna use the Lynx for a trade-in and she kinda laughed and said mister, you don't want that Lynx no more."

"Did you ask her why?"

"Yeah, she said she was on her way to pick up her kid at

the day-care center and she got there and the car just wouldn't leave. Said it started just fine, the motor run just fine, but she couldn't make it go into gear noway. So she called the service station and they come out there and looked at her and told her the transmission was plumb wore out. Well, you know the transmissions in them front-wheel drive cars."

I must have looked blank, because he went on. "You just cain't hardly get at them to work on them. She said the garage told her it would cost at least a thousand dollars to fix the transmission. Well, hell, the whole car ain't worth a thousand dollars, and even if she did get the transmission fixed the engine was still so bad she couldn't hardly drive uphill. So she said she junked it. Sold it to a junkyard for a hundred dollars. So I said lady, it sounds to me like you was damn lucky to win the New Yorker time you did, and she kinda laughed and said, well, yeah, maybe, but it was too big a car for her. Said she liked that little Chevy a lot better."

"So she took the Chevy out for a test drive," Millner said impatiently. "You still haven't told us its year or its license plate number or—"

Weaver looked at Millner reproachfully. "I gave that over the phone to this lady," he said.

"I already gave it to dispatch," I agreed. "Remember? I told you and you told Dub."

"I kinda wish you'd tell me what this is all about," Weaver added.

"It's about bank robbery and murder," Millner said precisely. "This woman is the accomplice of the two men who kidnapped and murdered a bank teller downtown on Saturday. They've now kidnapped another bank teller."

Weaver was standing with his mouth open. "You gotta be kidding—that nice little lady—"

"That nice little lady might not have pulled the trigger herself," I said, "and Saturday she might not have known she was going to be involved in murder, but she was there when the murder took place. So she darn sure knows it now. Mr. Weaver, if we got you and another person who saw the lady to sit down together with a police artist or something like that—"

I stopped. Weaver was shaking his head vigorously. "I cain't do nothing like that," he said.

"Most people think they can't," I agreed, "but—"

"You ain't hearing me," he said. "You're telling me that nice little lady is involved with murder. I just cain't believe that. And so I'm not going to—"

"See that New Yorker?" I interrupted. "Your 'nice little lady' didn't win that in a magazine contest. Don't you ever read the material they send out? They always let people have cash instead of cars, if they want it. So why would she take the car and then sell it? You know that expensive a car loses about a third of its value by the time it's driven off the lot. She'd take the cash. But there's another reason why we know she didn't win it in a magazine contest. It isn't—it wasn't—her car. This was Dorene Coe's car. Her husband bought it for her. Dorene Coe was a nice little lady too. She was nineteen. I saw her, when they were marching her out of the bank downtown at gunpoint before they killed her. She was scared. They tell me this teller that was kidnapped today was scared too. She isn't nineteen. She's about my age—forty-three—and she's got a husband and four children at home. They didn't figure, when Mama left the house this morning, that she wasn't going to come back—ever. Now, will you help us get her back?"

Weaver was looking like I'd hit him over the head with something hard and unyielding. Then, slowly, he nodded. "I'll see what I can do," he said. "But I'm telling you the truth, I ain't that good at describing people."

A brown van turned into the car lot, and Weaver turned to look at it. So did Millner and I. It was driven by Bob Castle, and it was, we knew, loaded down with cameras, evidence collection material, fingerprint kits, and the like.

Bob got out of the car and we introduced him to Weaver. "I want to talk to you a little before I do anything else," he said to Weaver, and Millner and I decided to have a brief conference of our own while that was going on. As we went in opposite directions, I could hear Bob asking "Now, how much have you handled—"

"What about that Lynx story?" Millner asked. "Do you s'pose it's true?"

"It could be," I said, and reminded him I too had been driving a blue Lynx. "I know it costs an arm and a leg to get the transmission worked on at all. It cost us nearly five hundred dollars to get work done that cost less than eighty dollars when Harry's truck needed it."

Millner took his glasses off and rubbed the bridge of his nose. "Wonder how many wrecking yards there are in Fort Worth?"

"In Tarrant County. In the Mid-cities. In Dallas. In—"

"Don't be so gloomy," he said. "They're hitting around here. There's a good chance—a real good chance—they live around here. And if you want a dead car towed off you don't call a wrecking yard thirty miles away. You call the closest wrecking yard you can find."

"Downtown. Northeast Tarrant County."

"Who's in the office?"

"How am I supposed to know who is in the office?" I demanded. "I'm not in the—"

"Deb," Millner said, "shut up and let me think."

In the end, we went into the little building—single wall construction, one room with two desks piled higher with paper than Robert Coe's dining-room table, one corner partitioned off to make a small, and filthy, rest room—to call the office. There was no earthly reason why it took a detective to telephone wrecking yards and ask about Lynxes that had been hauled in dead since Saturday. The secretary could do it well enough.

"Captain," I said after we hung up the phone, "when is this supposed to have happened?"

"When is what supposed to have happened?"

"This car breakdown. When is it supposed to have happened? She definitely had the Lynx on Saturday. She—"

"When those kids saw them at the park Sunday, what were they driving?"

"The New Yorker. But—"

"So? If you're going to rob a bank, do you take your kid with you?"

"I don't rob banks."

"Obviously. But if you were going to, would you take your kid with you, or park the kid in a day-care center?"

"Most day-care centers aren't open on Saturday and I don't think any of them are open on Sunday."

"Then when—"

"That's my point," I managed not to yell. "She had the Lynx on Saturday. She's supposed to have had the Lynx break down when she went to pick up her kid. Most day-care centers aren't open on Saturday. Almost none of them—probably none at all—are open on Sunday. Today's Monday and she might have taken her kid *to* a day-care center but she certainly hasn't—or hadn't—had time to pick the kid back *up*, and if the car died on the way *to* the center she didn't have time to sell it to a junk dealer by nine o'clock this morning."

"So it happened Saturday or it didn't happen," Millner clarified.

"Yeah. But most day-care centers—"

Millner picked up the phone again and called the secretary again. "Tell these junk dealers it probably happened Saturday," he said. "After you've done that, start calling day-care centers. Ask them if they're open on Saturday. If they are, ask them if they know if some woman's car broke down when the woman went to pick up her kid Saturday afternoon sometime."

We went outside then, to see Bob Castle in the act of photographing the car—front, back, both sides. This is SOP. He set the camera aside and opened the fingerprint kit, beginning, just as I would have done, with fingerprinting the driver's door.

There was, of course, nothing there. It had been

wiped—but she must have shut the door. How could she have wiped it without Weaver seeing?

Bob wondered the same thing. I know because he asked. Weaver, a bewildered expression on his face, shook his head. "No, of course she didn't wipe the door," he said. "But she was wearing driving gloves. Does that make any difference?"

It made some difference.

And very few people in this area wear driving gloves in this kind of weather.

We weren't looking now for Dorene Coe's fingerprints. We knew she'd been in this car; it was her car. But of course we had her prints for elimination. And that was good, because unless this car had been cleaned thoroughly there'd be a lot of her prints in it. We'd have to eliminate them, and her husband's prints, and then anything that was left might—might—belong to one of the two holdup men or to their star-struck female accomplice.

Might. Not necessarily would. Coe's insistence that he hadn't let Dorene have friends was very likely more guilt trip than fact. There was no guessing how many invited guests she might have had in the Chrysler.

And of course there is no way at all to tell sex from fingerprints. It might be true in general that a woman's prints are smaller than a man's, because in general a woman's hands are smaller than a man's, but a small man will of course have smaller hands than a large woman. And a large man with tapering fingers will have smaller prints than a small woman with spatulate fingers.

So any print in the car that wasn't made by either of the Coes could be—but couldn't be assumed definitely to be—that of any one of the three who had abducted and killed her.

Bob turned to open the door. It was locked. He swore, mildly, and asked Weaver for the keys. Weaver, his expression even more bewildered, replied, "Mister, I don't have them keys."

"Why don't you?"

Weaver turned, glanced comprehensively around the lot. "Mister," he said, "do I look like taking a brand-new car—a New Yorker at that—for a trade-in? You look. There ain't a thing on this lot newer than ten years old. I got no New Yorkers. I got one Cadillac. It's twenty years old. I don't have that kind of money. She wasn't going to sell the New Yorker to me. So what would I have kept the keys for?"

That made sense. But now the question was, did we—Millner and I—go and ask Coe for the extra set of keys he must have around the house somewhere? Or did we send Bob to do that? Or did we send a patrol car to do that? Or did we just send for the fire department and have them open the car for us?

That's the kind of small question that pops up all the time in this kind of business. Because, going to get the keys certainly wasn't Bob's job. But if we did it and—unlikely as it now seemed—the woman or one of her cohorts turned up to regain custody of the New Yorker, Bob wouldn't exactly be equipped to handle the problem. You don't fight a sawed-off shotgun with a fingerprint brush. But if we sent a patrol car to get the keys and bring them to us we'd have a marked car on this lot, which we didn't want to do right now, just in case somebody did decide to return for the New Yorker. If we called the fire department we'd have a fire truck, which also is sort of noticeable, and on top of that we'd do some damage to the car, which Robert Coe might not care about now but there was always the possibility that he, or his insurance company, might notice at some point in the future.

I don't know what you would do. I don't know what we would have decided to do, because we didn't have to do any of those things. Dutch Van Flagg got on the radio to announce himself leaving the bank, and Millner got on the radio and sent Dutch to go ask Coe for the keys.

Then we all stood around and sort of waited, and while we were waiting Bob busied himself with getting the photo montage kit out of his car and beginning to work with it and with Weaver.

When you think of picture montage kits you probably think of Identikit. I always do. This one isn't Identikit, though. Identikit works—or worked, I haven't seen it lately—with hand-drawn features, and I wouldn't guarantee to recognize my grandmother from one of the drawings it produces. This montage kit—I think it's from Sirchie but won't swear to it—works with photographic features. I can't imagine how the fellow put it together, it must have taken fifty years and five million photographs, but the pictures that are produced manage to look almost—not quite, but almost—like pictures of the person you're looking for. When we first got the kit Irene wanted to try it out on somebody so she got me to describe Harry. What emerged looked almost exactly like him, close enough he could have put a small copy of the picture on his ID badge at Bell Helicopter and probably nobody would have noticed the difference.

What emerged here did not look any more like the real Carrie Fisher than it did like the real Melanie Griffith. What emerged, in a surprisingly short time, was a picture of a rather long-faced blond woman, her hair straight and surfer style. She looked depressingly ordinary. I couldn't have guaranteed my ability to pick her out of a crowd with the picture in my hand.

Well, it was a start. When Bob got through here he'd head for University Chrysler-Plymouth and corner everybody who had seen the woman there, and see if they could improve any on the picture.

By the time he finished the picture Dutch had arrived with the key. "I told Coe I didn't know when we'd be able to release the car to him," Dutch reported, "and he said he didn't want the car. He said he wants us to keep it."

"What in the hell does he expect us to do with it?" Millner demanded.

"Damned if I know," Dutch said. "It won't even do for an undercover car—too flashy."

"He'll get over it," Bob said, and opened the car door.

Things get a little awkward at this stage. When you know your criminals—we call them suspects to meet legal requirements, but that's not what we mean—have been in a specific car, you have to vacuum the car with a special little hand vacuum with special filters in it. The reason for this is that the smallest piece of dust, hair, or pollen might prove to be evidentiary, so you want to collect it all. In this case we knew that the criminals had been in possession of the New Yorker part of Saturday, all of Sunday, and part of Monday. That meant there might be dust from their front driveway, hair from their pet poodle, any one of two dozen other things that would help not to locate them but to prove identity once they were located by other means. But the problem is this: You need to vacuum but you also need to fingerprint. If you vacuum first you might damage or even obliterate the fingerprints, but if you dust for fingerprints first then you're going to vacuum up an awful lot of your own fingerprint powder.

Every ident tech has his or her own way of handling that problem. Bob's way was first he vacuumed the floorboard and seat on the driver's side front, and then he fingerprinted that area, and then he moved to the passenger's side front, and then—well, you get the picture. It was thorough, methodical, and very, very time-consuming. What with one thing and another, I was still standing on the parking lot of Clean Harry's A-1 Used Cars at noon—Millner was long gone, leaving me with instructions to ride back in with Bob—with a sunburned nose, knowing exactly why unmilked cows go around making that horrendous noise they make.

Bob crawled out of the trunk of the car—yes, out of it; he'd been all the way in it, with me standing guard to be sure the lid didn't shut accidentally—and said, "Deb, would you get me some evidence bags?"

"What size?"

"Big ones," he said impatiently.

That should have been obvious. He had a pile of small

plastic bags, all neatly and properly labeled, over on the asphalt beside the clipboard that held all his notes. That was where his fingerprint lifts would have been too, if he had any, which unfortunately he did not. Now, at last, he was ready to start collecting larger items from the car.

There wasn't much to collect. A pair of sneakers, almost certainly Dorene's, in the backseat. Gloves and a Fort Worth Mapsco in the glove box. A Dallas Mapsco in the backseat floorboard. A rented videotape, never returned, on the dash. Ruined now, of course. She had inside parking. Probably she'd laid it on the dash so she'd remember to return it. I've done that myself. They'd never bothered to remove it from the dash. Three days of Texas sun, magnified through car windows, does a number on videotapes.

Probably, by now, Robert Coe had gotten two dozen telephone calls from the video store asking him to return the tape.

If—as I suspected—there were no fingerprints on it, I'd return it myself and explain what happened. Surely no video store would hold the man responsible for damage to a tape occurring when his wife was kidnapped and murdered. Of course he could afford to pay for it. But that wasn't the point.

"That's the lot of it," Bob said, tucking all the smaller plastic evidence bags into a large paper one. "What about the car?"

I shook my head. "We'd better put somebody on it, just in case," I said.

I should have decided that hours ago. Now we had to wait another hour, while we called the stakeout squad and got them to call somebody in and send that somebody out here. But at last Carlos Amado—his name translated approximately as Charles Lover-boy, and he hated it—showed up, to be briefed on the situation.

Then we had to wait a little longer while Bob and Carlos, who were fishing buddies, ran their mouths a little while.

Bob and I left. "Lunch?" Bob asked.

I shrugged. I would have preferred to be in my own car, to go my own way; Bob was the third person I'd driven with today, and I was getting giddy and hoping I hadn't left anything in somebody else's car. Oh, well, if I had, eventually they'd get whatever it was back to me. "Yeah, I guess," I said ungraciously.

There's this nice barbecue place right off Belknap. Coors. They use the same logo the beer people do. I don't exactly know how they get away with that. I mean, if the owner's name is Coors (I don't know if it is or not) then the beer people couldn't do much about him using the same name, but you'd think they'd object like crazy to the same logo. Oh, well, I suppose either they don't know about it—though you'd think their delivery drivers would tell them—or else they figure it's good advertising.

It's definitely good barbecue.

Over my protests, Bob insisted on us sitting in the area where they have the television. I hate that, not because of the television, which I don't particularly mind, but because it is even smokier than the rest of the place, which is quite smoky enough. Country music, barbecue, beer, and cigarettes seem to go together. I like the country music and the barbecue well enough, the beer I can do without, and the cigarettes—well. If Carrie Nation had burned tobacco fields instead of wrecking bars that would be just fine with me.

Bob did not agree. Bob lit a cigarette. I ostentatiously gagged. Bob ignored me. And the television said, "Do you know this woman?"

Well, well, well. So Irene did get through at the bank, and she decided not to wait for Bob to go to University Chrysler-Plymouth. She went herself.

The picture looked enough like the one Bob had produced for it to be obvious that it was the same woman. And there was a surprising amount of information about her. Not her name, of course; we still didn't have that. Presumably Millie was still on the phone to wrecking yards and day-care centers. But the woman's habit of visiting car dealers several times and then asking to take a car out for a few hours. The blue Lynx she might not have anymore. The fact that she might have a child, that her car might have broken down Saturday outside a day-care center—

Something was bothering me and I couldn't figure out what, but I was feeling more and more uneasy. "Bob," I said, "I want to go back to that used car lot."

"What for?"

"Because I want to."

"We haven't had lunch yet."

"Bob, I want to go back to that used car lot."

"Ah, Deb—"

"Then give me the car keys, and you can stay here and eat lunch."

A long time ago, a friend of mine was eating lunch. He wasn't my friend then because it was before I went on the police department. He was eating lunch with his partner, and they got a call. Just a little minor call, a disturbance at the bus station, somebody raising sand. They needed a policeman to go and remove the man. Nothing serious. So Billy said, "Let it wait till I finish my pie. It can't be that urgent."

But his friend was through eating. "You sit here and finish the pie," he said. "I'll go around and cover it and then swing back and pick you up."

So Billy finished his pie, but his friend never got back to pick him up.

I've heard a lot of descriptions of Billy, sitting on the steps of the emergency room crying while inside they were trying—with no hope at all—to keep his partner alive long enough for his wife to get there to see him one more time.

Bob knew that story as well as I did. He wouldn't let me go to Clean Harry's alone. I was shamelessly trading on that fact, and he knew I was doing it, and I could tell from the way he drove the car that he was mad at me. He knew I could tell it and he meant me to be able to tell it.

But that was before we got back to Clean Harry's and found all the glass shot out of the New Yorker, and the bodies of Harry Weaver and Carlos Amado lying in the driveway. Carlos had his service revolver in his hand. There was blood in the driveway a few feet away. So he'd clipped one of them. For all the good it didn't do.

Bob got out of the car and hooked the strobe up to the side of the camera and methodically began to take pictures of the bodies, trying to ignore the tears streaming down his face. I got on the radio.

· 6 ·

"SO WHAT DO THEY plan on doing next?" Captain Millner demanded savagely. "Kill the wrecking yard owner? Knock off the whole day-care center? What do these bastards plan on doing next?"

I shook my head. There wasn't much, if anything, left to say. Millner turned, got in his car, and drove off in the wake of the ambulances, without giving me a chance to ask for a ride with him.

At least the ambulances had gone since I was last here, about an hour ago. I no longer had to work at keeping my eyes averted from the shattered body of Carlos Amado, though the chalk outline, the blood and the bone and tissue fragments, still lay on the asphalt. The medical examiner had gone; there wasn't, after all, much of anything for him to do except pronounce the bodies dead, and that was pretty obvious. A sawed-off shotgun doesn't leave much doubt as to its intentions or its results.

All possible entrances to Clean Harry's (a name that had been funny, that was now grotesque) were roped off, with patrol officers standing guard. Bob and Irene were working inside the perimeter, not that there was one chance in a thousand of any useful physical evidence. You go through the motions. That's all. You go through the motions. Detectives were walking up and down both sides of the street trying to find somebody who had seen or heard something. I had been involved in that quest. I can tell you the results easily enough by describing my first interview, with the owner of a little mom-and-pop grocery directly across the street from Clean Harry's. "Lady, I didn't see nothing. I didn't hear nothing," he told me.

"Four shotgun blasts and two pistol shots this close—" I began incredulously.

"I didn't see nothing, I didn't hear nothing," he repeated. "Not so long as them bastards is still on the street I don't know nothing. You get 'em locked up and maybe I'll remember something. But now—no way. I got what you might call a strong sense of self-preservation."

I'd finished my side of the street with nothing better than that, and there was no use going to help cover somebody else's territory because they were all about through too. And nobody knew nothing. Nobody knew nothing. I'd returned to the scene to find something of a carnival atmosphere prevailing. Periodically a helicopter buzzed overhead; three television news crews and a varying, but always large, number of print and radio reporters came and went. A television anchorwoman adjusted her skirt, which was blowing a little in the breeze, adjusted her hair, which was doing the same, and then spoke into a microphone.

"A police spokesman has now provided official confirmation that Fort Worth Police Corporal Carlos Amado, twenty-seven, and used car salesman Harry Weaver, age not available, were shot to death early this afternoon at Clean Harry's A-1 Used Car Lot in Fort Worth. Details still are sketchy, and police have refused to explain the presence of the plainclothes officer at the car lot, though indications are that it is somehow related to the weekend abduction and murder of bank teller Dorene Coe, nineteen, of Fort Worth, and this morning's C&S Bank robbery that led to the abduction of teller Deandra Black. I'm Sonja Jensen, standing by at the scene to provide further details as they become available. We take you now—"

I don't know where she took us now. I quit listening. I had just noticed Nathan Drucker getting into his car, and if he was going into the station I wanted to go too. I had not, after all, been there since early this morning, and I was ready to go in. To start on my reports, which I was not going to finish tonight without staying late and I had no intention of staying late, and then to get in my car and go home.

Where I could cry in peace.

Carlos Amado had come on the police department when he was twenty-two. Five years. He'd worked uniform division the first year and I'd come across him now and then, the way you do uniform people, never really knowing them. Not in a department the size of this one. But he'd been in the stakeout squad four years and I'd seen a lot of him those four years. I couldn't really say we'd been close friends. But we'd been warm acquaintances.

His wife Bev worked at the downtown library. They'd tried to juggle their shifts so that one of them was at home with the two children most of the time. Of course it didn't always work; there were days like today, when he got called in while Bev was still at work. So he'd have taken the children by Bev's mother's house. That was how they did things. He'd told me about it once. He'd said they had a great life, he and Bev and the kids.

I supposed somebody had gone by the library and told Bev what had happened, had taken her home; somebody else had driven her car home because she was probably in no state at all to drive. I supposed somebody had called a priest for her; I remembered that Carlos was Catholic—and he'd died instantly, so that there had been no last rites for him, what kind of difference would that make? Not being a Catholic, I hadn't the slightest idea. I supposed I ought to go by this afternoon to talk with her, only I hadn't the slightest idea what to say.

"You okay, Deb?" Nathan asked.

I shrugged. "Yeah. You?"

"I guess."

He was just about exactly as all right as I was. And that wasn't very. To anyone who didn't know me I probably would appear perfectly calm, even inhumanly, unfeelingly calm considering the circumstances. Anybody who knew me would know better at a glance.

Nathan Drucker knew me. And I knew him.

"You ever get any lunch?" he asked.

"I don't want any."

"You've got to eat something."

"I'll eat eventually."

He pulled into the parking lot of a hamburger stand. The northeast Tarrant County area has been poorer in that regard since Goldenburger shut down, forcing us—me, anyway—to rely on chain hamburger places. Usually that bothered me. Today it did not. I simply did not care about hamburgers. Dairy Queen's or Whataburger's or Wendy's or whatever or whoever. I did not want a hamburger. I did not want anything to eat.

Nathan did not ask me what I wanted to eat. He went in while I sat in the car with the radio turned on. He came back with two bags and handed me one. It contained a hamburger, fries, and a chocolate malt.

"Nathan, I told you I didn't want—"

"I don't either. Now eat it. You making yourself sick isn't going to bring Carlos back."

He was right, of course, and I knew quite well that Carlos would be saying the same thing if it were Nathan dead. Nathan was eating his hamburger. He looked about as interested in it as I was in mine. I shrugged and started to eat.

And the radio came alive. This is not to say it had been

silent before; it had not been. A police radio is rarely if ever silent. But people who are around police radios all day learn not to hear the radio at all unless it is saying something that person needs to hear. Thus, any police officer hears whatever signal or code means "robbery in progress" or "officer needs help" in that area; other than that about all anybody is likely to hear is his or her own call signal.

Which was what I heard. My own signal. I was needed in the police station. "En route," I said, and Nathan handed me his malt to hold while he backed out of the parking lot. I handed it back when he got out onto the road, and both of us still had unfinished malts when we got into the detective bureau.

To find that the briefing room on the detective floor was totally full. The robbery squad. The homicide squad. The major case squad. Several FBI agents, not just Dub and Chang but also Darren Fletcher and two or three others I didn't know or didn't know well. A Texas Ranger. There also were four very well-dressed men I had never seen before. All four came equipped with expensive and exotic cowboy boots—the kind real cowboys wouldn't be caught dead wearing—and LBJ-style white Stetsons and very fancy briefcases. They didn't look like the boots and white Stetsons type. They did look like the expensive briefcase type.

Sergeant Distefano, who heads the special details unit, was there also. We in the detective bureau are more likely to refer to his crew as the stakeout squad, because we more often call on the unit for stakeouts than for anything else. Not surprisingly, Distefano—Carlos Amado's supervisor—was somewhat red about the eyes.

It seemed we were having a Meeting.

Millner gazed pointedly at my paper cup and I dropped it as unobtrusively as possible, which wasn't very, into the closest trash can and found a seat. Drucker did not drop his paper cup into the trash can. He went right on drinking from it. I wasn't surprised. He'd already made his philosophy on this matter clear.

The men I didn't recognize turned out to be from the Texas Banking Commission. What the Texas Banking Commission expected to be able to do about the robberies that we weren't already doing was a little vague to me, but then people on major committees are like that. Mainly they want to know what we have done and what we are doing. It does not occur to them that what we are doing is having a meeting with them when we could be out working on solving the case.

Millner, who as usual in this sort of situation assumed the role of chairman, began by reviewing the situation. The first robbery Saturday. Descriptions of suspects. Detective work. Description of blond Harrison Ford fan. Finding of the body Sunday. The teenagers who told us about the shooting. The second robbery Monday. How I'd located Harry Weaver, what Harry Weaver had told me, what had happened to Harry Weaver and Carlos Amado. The guard that had been placed on Connie Daynes, the saleswoman at University Chrysler-Plymouth. This was the first I'd heard of that. I hoped it would do some good. The lookout on the white Chevy that had been taken from A-1. The lookout on Deandra Black and her beige Honda Accord, of which we now had the year and license plate number. The still-continuing search for the wrecking yard the Lynx had been taken to if the woman's story was true, which it probably was, because if it wasn't what earthly reason would they have had for shooting Weaver? The still-continuing search for the day-care center that was open on Saturday, where a blue Lynx had died.

Those telephone calls, by the way, were getting a little hairy, because until this meeting had been convened secretaries had still been concentrating on getting written statements from witnesses to the robbery and kidnapping this morning. Since they couldn't get the statements by themselves—the statements being presumably and legally made to police officers—the remaining witnesses were now cooling their heels in the halls and conference rooms, because the detectives were now in this meeting. But while the secretaries were taking statements they couldn't be calling wrecking yards and day-care centers and while they were calling day-care centers and wrecking yards they couldn't be taking statements.

We had borrowed some more secretaries from other parts of the building.

He told about the blood that said Carlos had hit one of them. About the phone calls to hospitals, to see if anyone had come in with a gunshot wound. He told about—

"But what are you doing about all of it?" demanded one of the banking commissioners, who bore an unfortunate resemblance to John Tower dressed as John Connally.

"I just told you what we're doing about it," Millner responded with something approaching patience.

"That doesn't sound like very much to me."

"Then what else would you suggest we do?" Millner inquired.

"That's your job, not mine."

"Precisely. It is my job. And—"

And the door opened. "Captain Millner?" Millie shouted. "Robbery in progress, First Security Bank."

This was ridiculous. These had to be stupid robbers.

I don't know what the banking commissioners did. All the rest of us went out the door as fast as that many people could get through one door. We did not stop for elevators; we went tearing down the stairs and poured into cars with very little regard for who went with whom—that was how I happened this time to wind up in the car with a Texas Ranger named Neal Ryan. I know Neal pretty well. He's a bookish-looking man with nothing much about him that fits the traditional concept of a Texas Ranger except his hand-tooled leather boots, which in his case *are* the kind a real cowboy would wear. When he is in court he wears a suit and tie; when he is not in court he wears the same kind of wash-and-wear gray chino work clothes you'd see on any delivery man, the kind straight from the pages of the Sears catalog. The five-pointed star in a circle pinned to the gray chino work shirt would say "Ranger" to any Texan, and the six-inch barrel on the Colt Cobra on his hip says this and that too. What it says is not likely to be forgotten.

As the car roared out of the garage Neal turned on his siren and flipped a switch that turned on the blue light on his dash and simultaneously caused his headlights to turn on and change rapidly from high to low, high to low. This is far more noticeable in traffic than you might think if you have never seen it. He flipped another switch, to turn his radio from state to city of Fort Worth. The dispatcher was in midsentence. "Is covered. All units, slow down, situation is covered."

There were fewer sirens in the air than there had been a moment before. But not all sirens cut off. Ours didn't. I glanced at Neal and he said blandly, "I don't work for the city of Fort Worth." Implied, but not stated, was the rest of it. "I drive as fast as I want to."

A uniformed officer and a bank guard stood on either side of a somewhat frightened-looking, and somewhat scroungy-looking, man in his mid-thirties. As I said, they were standing. He was sitting.

It's not as easy as one might think to guess the height of a sitting person. But he was going to be over six feet. His clear-olive skin was lightly tanned, his black hair was a little long, his mustache was a little shaggy, and his blue eyes were very, very angry. He was wearing blue jeans and a white T-shirt. The T-shirt had a logo of three reptilian fingers circling a globe, and under it, in quotation marks, was the phrase To Life Immortal! It was fairly easy to guess that he, like my son Hal, was a War of the Worlds fan.

But most likely he was not being so eagerly guarded

because he liked to watch television shows about Martians who turned out not to be Martians at all, but rather creatures from a galaxy far, far away.

"What's going on?" I asked.

The guard and the police officer stared at me. "Police business," the officer said gruffly.

This happens every so often. This department has gotten too darn big. "Detective Deb Ralston, Major Case Squad, Fort Worth Police Department," I said. "Now what's going on?" I could see no signs of an attempted holdup, but at this stage looks could be deceiving.

"You know that holdup Saturday?" the officer asked me.

"I am quite well acquainted with that holdup Saturday," I said.

"Doesn't he look to you like the videotape?"

I looked at the man. He looked at me. "That was a very fuzzy videotape," I said.

"That's what I tried to tell them," the man said bitterly. "Look, I just come in here to open an account, for cryin' out loud, and all of a sudden this teller starts screaming and then these guards was on me like shit on a shingle."

"He looks just like the videotape," the patrol officer, whose name tag read Hickson, said stubbornly. "And he's dressed just like it too."

"There were two men on the videotape," I pointed out. "Neither was wearing a T-shirt. They were both wearing T-shirts in the holdup this morning, but neither shirt had a logo on it. Which one do you think he looks just like?"

"The tall one. He's the right size. I got him to sign a Miranda form." He handed it over, with approximately the same expression my dog gets when he has just rolled in some particularly noxious odor.

"I seen the videotape too," the man said. "The dude had a mask on. How am I supposed to look just like somebody nobody even saw?"

"I saw him," I commented. "And I don't mean on the videotape."

"Then you know it wasn't me."

"Actually I don't know it. Yet. What's your name?"

"Nick Casavetes."

Another movie star name, I thought with some interest. Well, the last name, anyway.

"Mr. Casavetes, would you mind standing up?"

"Sure. If I can go home afterward." He stood up. "Now you know it wasn't me."

I looked him over. I still couldn't say it wasn't him. I couldn't honestly say he had been the man in the bank Saturday, but I couldn't say he hadn't been either.

"Was he armed?" I asked Hickson.

"Hell, no, I wasn't armed," Casavetes said. "Why do I need a gun to open a checking account?"

"No, he wasn't armed," Hickson said.

"Did you run him on NCIC?"

"Yes," Hickson said. "No wants." He did not say no records, an omission that might—or might not—be significant, depending on Hickson's degree of experience, which I suspected was less than absolutely terrific.

Neal, who had strolled off somewhere, strolled back. "I asked for a private place where we could talk," he said. "Seems banks don't *have* private places anymore. Everything's out in the open so everybody can see everybody."

Casavetes looked at him. "Who the hell are you?"

"Neal Ryan. Texas Ranger."

"Yeah?" Casavetes said, with the first real interest he'd shown in anything other than his own predicament. "I didn't know there were any Rangers anymore."

"'Said the youth to the world, sir, I exist,'" Neal said, and this time Casavetes and I both stared at him.

"Yes, there are Rangers," Neal said. "Yes, I'm one of 'em. Let's you and me and Detective Ralston go out and sit in my car and see if we can get this straightened out."

His car was a little better for that kind of straightening out than a city police car would have been, although several city police cars had arrived by now, because its backseat wasn't caged off and it had its impedimenta—shotguns and the like—stowed more neatly. Ten minutes later, Casavetes and I were sitting in the backseat and Neal and Captain Millner were in the front seat. "Well," Neal said, "who wants to start this?"

"Am I under arrest?" Casavetes asked.

"No, sir, you are not under arrest," Captain Millner said. "However, I do want to warn you that anything you say—"

"Yeah, yeah, yeah, I know all that," Casavetes interrupted. "That cop inside, he told me that and had me sign this sheet of paper."

"I've got it," I said, and Millner nodded.

"If I'm not under arrest can I leave?"

"Not exactly," Millner said.

"Then if I can't leave I'm under arrest."

"You are being detained for questioning," Neal said.

"Is that legal?"

"Probably," Millner said.

"What the hell do you mean, probably?" Casavetes demanded. "Either it's legal or it's not legal. And it doesn't look very legal to me."

"Let's put it this way," I said. "Nobody wants to arrest you right now. Right now we want to ask you some questions. You don't have to answer them. But you've been identified by at least one person as having been involved in two robberies, two kidnappings, and one murder. The other kidnap victim is still missing. Now, as I said, we don't want to arrest you. But you can see for yourself that we can't just turn you loose until we're satisfied that it was a case of mistaken identity. So if you want to answer questions without being arrested, fine. If you don't, well, we'll have to think a little bit about what we want to do next."

"I thought in this country a man was innocent till proven guilty. And you can't prove me guilty of something I didn't do. But what if I can't prove I'm innocent?"

"This conversation is not off to a good start," I said.

"You're telling me? It got off to a real bad start about the time that goon in the bank started waving that gun at me."

"Just let me ask some questions, okay?" I said, my mind involuntarily flashing to Carlos dead on the asphalt with two-thirds of his chest blown away, while I had to be polite to the man who might have shot him not just because the man might not be the one who had shot him, but also because you have to be polite to suspects. I would be expected to be polite to Casavetes if I had seen him kill Carlos.

Something in my voice must have warned Casavetes it was time to quiet down, because he shrugged. "Okay. Ask your questions."

"You said you were in the bank to open an account, right?"

"Right."

"Any reason you picked this particular bank?"

"Any reason why I shouldn't?"

"Not that I know of. Where do you live?"

"Arlington."

"You live in Arlington but you're opening an account at a bank in downtown Fort Worth? Where do you work?"

"Euless." His voice sounded sullen.

"You live in Arlington and you work in Euless and you're opening an account at a bank in downtown Fort Worth?"

"So I'm gonna move to Fort Worth in about six months and I want to open an account now so my checks will say when the account was opened. You ever try to cash checks on a new account in a new community? If you have it ought to make sense to you."

"What kind of work do you do?"

"I build boats." He was smirking a little and I couldn't see why. Whether or not he was guilty, he wasn't doing a very good job of convincing me or anybody else he was innocent.

But, as he said, that wasn't his job. It was mine to prove him guilty—if he was guilty.

"Where were you Saturday morning?"

"What time Saturday morning?"

"Oh, any time at all," I said vaguely.

He sighed elaborately. "I got up at eight-thirty and ate some Cheerios and watched Bullwinkle on TV. How's that?"

It happens that my son Hal is an enormous Bullwinkle fan. If Bullwinkle were on TV on Saturday morning he would be watching it. He does not. Which to my mind definitely and conclusively proves that Bullwinkle is not on TV on Saturday morning in the Fort Worth viewing area.

Of course I'd have to check that with a copy of *TV Guide*. But I was going to be right.

I did not tell Casavetes that Bullwinkle is not on the air on Saturday mornings. I just said, "What did you do after that?"

"I went to the lot and got a boat and went to Lake Dallas and stayed there the rest of the day."

"What lot?" Captain Millner asked.

"The boat lot. Where I work. There's this boat employees can use if they want to."

"So you went to the boat lot and you got a boat and went to Lake Dallas the rest of the day," I said. "Anybody go with you?"

"This girl."

"What girl?"

"Just this girl. I met her at this bar."

"What's her name?"

"Look, you're not going to go talk to her, are you?" Casavetes said nervously. "Because her old man, he'll kill me."

"That'll teach you to hang around with married women," Neal said.

"Not that kind of old man," Casavetes said. He wriggled a little and said, "Oh, hell. This girl, she's sixteen."

"And you met her at a bar?" Millner inquired. "Seems to me I ought to know more about this bar."

"Well . . . Okay, I didn't meet her at a bar. I met her at this high school football game last fall. She's a kinda cute chick but her old man don't want her running around with nobody my age so she kinda sneaks around . . ."

"Name?" Neal repeated.

"Oh, hell. It's Rita Cleveland."

"And where does Rita Cleveland live?"

He gave an address in Bedford. "But you're not going to go out there—"

"We'll see," I said. "What's her phone number? We might not have to go out there."

He gave a phone number.

"Okay," I said. "Now this morning."

"What about this morning?"

"Where were you this morning?"

"I was at work. Where the hell do you think I'd be on Monday morning?"

"I don't know where you'd be," I said. "That's why I asked."

"Well, I was at work."

"Then how come you're not at work Monday afternoon?" Neal asked.

"I took off. Do I got to work all the time?"

"Most people work Monday afternoon," I said. "But if you don't that's between you and your boss. Tell me the name of the boat company."

"Presto."

"The name of the boat company is Presto?"

"That's what I said."

I wrote it down. "Now tell me its phone number."

"I don't know its phone number. You think I go around calling myself?"

"Who would I talk with to confirm you were at work?"

"My boss. Lonzo Hambley."

"You stay here with the Ranger while I go make a

phone call," I said, and got out of the car. Millner got out right behind me.

"What if Lonzo Hambley's the other one?" he asked me.

"I thought of that too," I said. "You know Bullwinkle's not on the air Saturday morning, don't you?"

"I'll admit I didn't know that," he said. "But I sort of had a suspicion about it. Well." He looked back toward the car. "He's looking good."

"He is except for one thing," I said.

"What's that?"

"During the robbery, the tall one did most of the talking," I said. "Not all of it, but most of it. And—I won't say I could certainly recognize his voice. But I think I could. And that doesn't sound like it."

Millner took off his glasses and rubbed the bridge of his nose. "Hmmm," he said. "Well. Go call, anyway."

Monday afternoon. What time? Almost four o'clock. I might catch Rita Cleveland at home and then again I might not.

One thing I was sure of: Rita Cleveland was not our star-struck blond. Every person who'd told me about her had agreed she was in at least her mid-thirties if not older.

On second thought I didn't want to telephone Rita Cleveland. I wanted to go and look at her while I was asking questions. Because I had a sort of a hunch that a sixteen-year-old who'd lie to her father to date a scrounge like Nick Casavetes would lie to me too. At least over the phone. She might not find it quite so easy to lie to me face-to-face.

Not that she wouldn't try it. But she might be a little less likely to succeed.

So I called the operator and got the telephone number for Presto Boats in Arlington and then, because phone booths don't have metro lines (that's the special telephone line that lets people call all over the Dallas-Fort Worth metroplex without any long-distance charges), I got my little telephone credit card out of my purse and dialed the

Arlington number and dialed my own telephone number with all the little codes, so that the call would get billed to me. I'd turn in a request for reimbursement later if I remembered to. Right now getting reimbursed for a dollar phone call didn't seem very important. Not compared to Carlos Amado. Not compared to Dorene Coe.

Not compared to Deandra Black, who might still be alive.

The bell rang twelve times before it was answered by a rough male voice. I could hear what sounded like a power saw running in the background. "Yeah?"

"Is this Presto Boats?" I asked.

"Yes'm, this is Presto Boats."

"I'm calling about Nick Casavetes—"

I did not expect the response I got. The rough voice shouted, "You can tell that son of a bitch he's fired!" And the receiver slammed down in my ear.

Gingerly I went through the dialing procedure again. The same voice answered, this time on the second ring. "Yeah?"

"I'm Detective Deb Ralston, Fort Worth Police Department," I said hastily, "and I need some information about Nick Casavetes."

"Well, why didn't you say that to start with? What kinda information you need?"

"Was he at work this morning?"

"Yeah. He come in two hours late, but he was here."

"What time is he supposed to come in?"

"Eight. And he come in at ten."

"You sure it wasn't later than ten?"

"I watched him punch in. It was five minutes to ten."

Nine-thirty to five minutes to ten. From Belknap Road almost downtown to the city of Euless. Unless this man was his accomplice, and I didn't think now that he was, Nick Casavetes was clear. But . . . "What about Saturday?" I asked.

"What do you mean, what about Saturday?"

"Did he take a boat out Saturday?"

"Yeah, probably. Somebody did and he takes 'em out a lot."

"Do you have any record of what time he took it out and brought it back?"

"No'm, I don't. Say, what is this about?"

"Just checking on something," I said vaguely. "Would you be willing to tell me why you've decided to fire him?"

"He ain't here, is he? How'm I supposed to run a business when half my employees decide for themselves when they want to work and when they don't?"

"But you're sure he arrived there this morning at five minutes to ten?"

"Lady, I got his time card and I watched him punch in. Punched back out at eleven-thirty for lunch and ain't been back since. That's the sort of guy that gives lazy a bad name. Except for one thing."

"What's that?" I asked.

"When he does work he's a damn—'scuse me, ma'am. When he does work he's a real good worker. I guess I won't fire him this time. Just tell him to get his ass—his tail back down here. He can work tonight to make up for the afternoon."

"Thank you," I said, and returned to the car. "Your boss says to tell you to get your tail back to work," I said. "That was after he fired you and then unfired you."

"Yeah, he does that," Casavetes said smugly. "He can't find nobody that works better than me."

I waited a minute. "So go," I told him.

He got out of the car and we watched him walk off with that expression any experienced cop—and most mothers—recognize easily. The expression of somebody who thinks he's getting away with something.

"You sure he's clear?" Millner asked me.

"Unless he can get from the C&S Bank to Euless in less than twenty-five minutes, he's clear," I said. "I'll still go talk to Rita Cleveland in the morning. But he's clear. At least for that."

"What do you mean?" Neal asked.

"I already told Millner," I said. "He wasn't watching Bullwinkle on TV Saturday morning. It wasn't on. He was doing something he would prefer we didn't know about."

"You got his identification?" Millner asked.

I nodded. "Hickson got it and gave it to me."

"I'm going to run him on NCIC again," Millner said. "I want a real good look at his record. I swear that son of a bitch is up to something."

We'd had the radio off. You don't question a robbery suspect with a radio interrupting. Neal turned it back on now and asked for developments.

There weren't any developments.

Carlos Amado was still dead.

Deandra Black, middle-age mother of four, was still missing.

Neal dropped me by my car and I went home. Without making reports. And Millner actually let me get away with it.

· 7 ·

THE GINGHAM DOG AND the calico cat side by side on the table sat, the table being the picnic table, which Hal and Lori (it couldn't possibly have been Harry) had for some unknown reason seen fit to haul from the backyard into the front yard. Of course Pat is definitely not made out of gingham. The cat is not made of calico, but she is a calico cat. When I got out of the car Pat, who rather likes to show off, nosed at the cat. His request was eloquent: "Run so I can chase you."

The cat yawned very widely, displaying her tongue, the pink-and-black mottled roof of her mouth, and about five hundred of her teeth. Her reply was equally clear: "I do not choose to run."

Pat cast a frustrated, and rather befuddled, glance at me. "I can't do anything about it," I told him.

As I proceeded toward the front door the cat jumped off the table and halfheartedly began to jog. Pat scrambled down and went after her, and she promptly shot up the mesquite tree, which was only about four feet from the picnic table. Pat sat down abruptly and gazed up into the mesquite tree. He certainly couldn't get up it. I had no idea how he had managed to get on top of the picnic table; he is a very strong dog, but he is not at all athletic.

This is not only a baby-teasing cat. It also is a dog-teasing cat.

Inside, Cameron, rather to my surprise considering the time of day, was not howling. Hal and Lori were playing some kind of Nintendo game on the TV, and they had thoughtfully hauled the playpen in front of the TV set between them. Cameron seemed utterly entranced by the colors, the blips, and the sound effects.

Harry did not have his radios on; apparently he didn't feel like competing with the video game. He was sitting on the couch reading his newest survivalist junk mail, a Brigade Quartermaster's catalog, and he got up and said, "I'm sorry, babe."

Of course I burst into tears.

Hal and Lori turned off the video game and started to slink away into Hal's room. This of course caused Cameron to commence howling. I picked him up and sat down on the couch.

Lori has not, by the way, moved in with us. But her mother, a police officer and widow of another police officer, was away for a three-week course at the Texas State Police Academy in Austin. Hal and Lori had presented many, to them, exemplary arguments as to why Lori should spend those three weeks with us, occupying what had been Vicky and Becky's room before they got married and moved out, but Lori's mother and I presented more and stronger arguments as to why that would be a very, very, very bad idea. We won on the basis of parental authority, not on the basis of logic, which no teenager ever concedes. But anyway Lori was staying with an aunt. The aunt lived six blocks from us and Lori never went over there until the last possible moment.

So I was seeing far more than usual of Lori this week, and even usual is quite a lot.

Five-thirty. Cameron was going to request his supper in about half an hour. Carrying him, I went to check the pantry and refrigerator to see what I could think of that required little or no cooking for the rest of the family, so that I could start on that before sitting down with the baby.

"You don't have to do that," Harry said, noticing where I was headed. "I was going to take us out for supper."

"I don't want to be taken out to supper, thank you."

"I mean I was going to ask Hal and Lori to baby-sit Cameron while you and I went out to supper," he amplified.

"I have a Scout meeting," Hal bellowed from his room. Where the conversation concerns him, that kid has ears like a—like a—like an African elephant.

"I can baby-sit Cameron," Lori said, hurrying into the living room. She is becoming alarmingly maternal at times.

"What do you mean you have a Scout meeting?" I demanded. "You never have Scouts on Monday night." Hal's Scout troop is sponsored by the LDS Church. The LDS Church has proclaimed that Monday night is Family Night and families are supposed to spend Monday night doing things together. Therefore it does not hold any other meeting on Monday night. In our family this was, at best, a joke. Partly, but not only, because Hal was the only Mormon in the family. There were also these factors like Harry going to call bingo (Elks Lodge, White Settlement Road, Monday and Thursday nights) and me getting called out for all kinds of nasty crimes (often murder) at all kinds of idiotic hours. And people who kill each other do it without the least consideration as to what police prefer to do at that particular time.

"Tonight we have a Scout meeting on Monday night," Hal said. "I don't know why."

"But I'm not going to bingo," Harry said hastily.

The telephone rang. Probably Harry was about to find out he was going to bingo after all.

It was Lori's aunt requesting Lori's presence at supper. A brief argument was ineffective, and Hal left in the pickup truck to drive Lori home. Obviously she could walk the six blocks, and frequently did (in fact they both frequently did), but that wasn't the point. It would have been in some subtle way I as a woman am not equipped to understand unmasculine for Hal to let Lori walk home for supper.

I went on trying to think of something for our supper.

"You don't have to do that," Harry said again. "I'll go out and bring something in. Chinese? Pizza?"

"Why does everybody keep trying to *feed* me!" I shrieked quite unfairly, and Harry of course looked hurt.

"I'm sorry," I said. "I'm just not hungry. I had lunch real late. I'm trying to think of something for you and Hal."

"Hal and I," Harry said, "can have peanut butter sandwiches. Why don't you go get some rest?"

"I've got to feed the baby," I said.

"I can feed the baby." I didn't say anything, and after a minute Harry said. "Oh. Yeah. Go feed the baby."

The phone rang again. There are times I want to take that phone and throw it in the Trinity River.

This time it was for Harry, and although I could hear only half the conversation the half I could hear was quite informative. "No. No, I wasn't going to— But— Then get Frank— Oh, hell."

Harry hung up with a frustrated expression.

"You have to go call bingo," I said.

"Jerry was supposed to call and he got stuck late at work. They can't call Frank because he's got laryngitis. But I'll only call till Jerry gets there. It shouldn't be long. Then I'll bring you supper. Don't cook anything."

I had no difficulty at all promising not to cook anything. With that assurance, Harry departed.

Hal returned from transporting Lori, and began in a

great hurry to put on his Scout uniform, which is replete with medals and ribbons and stuff, most of which I have watched him get and few of which have had any noticeable effect on his day-to-day conduct. From his bedroom, I could hear a monologue, slightly muffled by the bedroom door, which seemed to be addressed at me. "I told 'em I can't have the truck on Monday because my dad needs it so Ronnie's gonna come pick me up—"

The phone rang again.

They had found Deandra Black's 1987 beige Honda Accord, parked in the area that once a year holds the Fort Worth Fat Stock Show and the rest of the time houses things like my second-favorite flea market (my most favorite flea market, of course, being the one in Grand Prairie) and various events of various types.

They had not found Deandra Black.

They requested my presence.

I told the dispatcher I'd talk to her later, and then I called Captain Millner, hoping I could catch him before he went out the door. I did. "My husband is away. My son is about to leave for a Scout meeting. How do you expect me to go to a crime scene and do anything useful while carrying a ten-week-old baby?"

"Get a baby-sitter."

"Oh, sure! In five minutes?"

"Get a baby-sitter who can be on call when you have call-outs," Captain Millner said. "Or request transfer to uniform division where you'll have fewer call-outs."

That wasn't an option and he knew it as well as I did. I am good at my work and I like it, except when I have a baby.

I hung up and turned to Hal.

His expression was quite alarmed. "Mom, I gotta go to this Scout meeting!"

"Fine, you can do your good turn for the day while you're at Scouts."

Was that unfair, or was that unfair?

But Hal had calmed down a lot lately.

Of course it was unfair. To Cameron and me as well as to Hal. But I had a hunch that a group of teenage boys who might pretend horror at the presence of a baby, if their mothers and girlfriends were around, would be quite enthralled with that same baby in the absence of female presence.

At least I told myself I had such a hunch. But I still felt like a worm.

I prepared the diaper bag and made sure Hal had his door key in his pocket, and then I left fast pretending I didn't know I was crying again.

I am a wet dishrag. I am an overflowing sponge. I am a waterfall, a raincloud. The doctor says it's because of fluctuating hormone levels in my body as a result of childbirth and it'll let up eventually. It better. It is driving me nuts and it is driving every male around me nuts, especially in view of the fact that they seem to think it is a weapon rather than a reaction.

Anyway, I quit crying by the time I got into traffic.

You know those three long display buildings that house the flea market? Well, actually only one and sometimes two of them house the flea market, but there are three of them like barracks buildings with their long ends parallel and their short ends facing the road. Across the street from them are some parallel parking spots where I usually manage to find a place when I am going to the flea market. The Accord was in one of those slots. Nobody had noticed it during the day, but that didn't mean it wasn't there. A lot of people park in that area during the day, and as it's unmetered, there is just no reason to notice. It had become noticeable in the evening, when no other cars had any reason at all to be there, and a reasonably alert patrol officer found it.

Routine. Routine. Routine.

We have a new ident tech, Sarah Collins. I've met her before when she was in uniform division, but I'd never encountered her at a crime scene before and had no idea how good she might or might not be. In fact, it had crossed my mind to wonder if she'd been put in ident because she had been studying and would be good at it, or whether it was because she was just flat too pretty to be on the street. She has a very unusual ethnic mix—black, white, and Oriental—and she's gotten the best parts of each race. Beige skin with a rosy overtone. Delicate high cheekbones. Green eyes. Reddish hair with just enough friz that it always looks as if she has a very good curly perm. I've seen her get wolf whistles when she was walking down the street in uniform carrying a shotgun.

She followed the same routine Irene or Bob would have followed. Photographs. Fingerprints outside. Open the door—this one wasn't locked, fortunately.

It wasn't locked, but there was blood on the front passenger's seat. Was that from Deandra Black? Or was this the car they'd driven to kill Weaver and Carlos? Could we be so lucky that this blood came from one of the suspects?

Very carefully and precisely, using bandage scissors, wearing plastic gloves (which have become a very much enforced SOP when working around blood, since the advent of AIDS) Sarah cut out the entire bloodstained area of the seat cover and laid it flat on nonabsorbent plastic to air-dry. Using forceps, she pulled out all of the blood-soaked padding and cushioning and put it on a sheet of plastic in a cardboard box. She did not seal any of that in evidence bags; if it had been sealed it would have begun to rot in a matter of hours. Left open to the air, it would air-dry and very little damage would be done to its evidentiary value. That is the theory; that is how it is done in small police departments that might not get their stuff to the lab for several days. In practice, Sarah would take this straight to the medical examiner's office on Camp Bowie, just a few blocks from here. It would never go to the police station at all, because the ME's office would retain it until it was time to present it in court, and then when all court procedures were finally and definitely finished with, the ME's office would, in a proper and sanitary manner, destroy the evidence.

With all of that dealt with, Sarah proceeded to collect everything on the floorboards and in the seat. Most of it probably belonged to Deandra and her family, but there was always the possibility that something might not. She vacuumed, using the special little filters. She fingerprinted the inside of the car.

And hallelujah, on the back—not the front—of the rearview mirror she collected the prints of a right index, right middle, and right ring finger.

Big prints. Almost certainly the prints of a man.

If they had been Deandra's husband's prints almost certainly Deandra would have obliterated them the next time she adjusted the mirror to suit herself. Besides that we already knew Mr. Black had his own car and said he never drove Deandra's car.

They had finally slipped. One of the bastards had slipped. In the excitement of the moment, of killing two men, of one of them getting hit, one of them—presumably the other, the one who had not been hit—forgot one of the places he touched.

We had something to search. And clearly Sarah was going to be a competent ident tech, though at the moment she still lacked a little in experience.

Grinning like the Cheshire cat, she asked, "Anything else I need to check before I take these in and get to work?"

"The trunk," I said, and Sarah answered, "Oops."

We had—at this time—no reason to suppose that Deandra Black was in the trunk.

We also had no reason to suppose that Deandra Black was not in the trunk.

The keys weren't with the car. Sarah and I hauled the backseat out to get through to the trunk that way.

Deandra was not in the trunk. There was no indication whatever that the robbers had ever opened the trunk.

I ordered the car towed to the pound. Then I got in my car and drove off, knowing that Sarah, unless she got more calls, would spend the rest of her shift methodically going through files searching for three fingerprints that matched those fingerprints, and that tomorrow Irene would fax them to the FBI for computer search.

Sarah had one more advantage. All three of those prints were whorls. That meant that the fingerprint classification was not 1/1, which takes in over half of all fingerprints, and it wasn't 5/17, which is about the next most common. It could be 25/9 or it could be anything from 25/9 up to 32/32, which is as high as primary classifications go. Just knowing that had ruled out almost two-thirds of all the fingerprints in file.

If I were Sarah I would check 32/32 first and work toward the front of the file. But I'm not Sarah.

Yes, I have been studying fingerprints during my leave of absence. I have been thinking that maybe I might want to go back into ident because they keep ident people on duty around the clock, which means that unless things get pretty hairy ident people don't get called in. Anymore. That is not the way it was when I was in ident.

But I probably won't do it.

The department probably wouldn't let me do it if I asked to. I am too useful where I am.

I was almost to the church. At this point the question became, which door was unlocked? It was not the front door. It was not—

It was not any of the doors. They were all locked. So I went to the door closest to the Relief Society room—that's the women's group, but for some reason that I do not pretend to understand, Scouts also hold their meetings there, carefully packing away the pretty framed needlepoint daisies and replacing that picture with a framed copy of the Scout law. I shook the door two or three times and then banged on it until somebody heard me and came and opened the door from the inside.

I removed Cameron, who seemed extremely happy to have a Tenderfoot badge safety-pinned to his diaper shirt, and went home.

Harry came home twenty minutes later, bringing Kentucky Fried Chicken, which I did not want but decided I had better tactfully eat anyway. By that time I had formulated a plan. It was, I felt, a very good plan. I would not be neglecting Harry or Cameron because they would be with me and besides that Cameron, like just about every baby I have ever met, loves to ride in the car. I would not be neglecting Hal because he was at a Scout meeting anyway. I would not be neglecting Deandra Black. And because I would not be neglecting anybody who needed my attention, I would not be neglecting myself and I would be in a good mood and I would feel great. "Harry," I said as guilelessly as possible, having eaten as little chicken as I thought I could get away with, "I'd like to go for a ride in the pickup truck."

He looked at me. "You're up to something," he said.

This man knows me.

I decided to abandon pretense. After all, this was for a good cause.

"I want to go look for Deandra Black," I said. "The pickup truck is up higher than this little tail-dragger car I've got so I can see better. Anyway if you're driving and I'm looking I can see—"

"Uh-huh," Harry said. "And just where do you intend to look for Deandra Black? I mean, Tarrant County is a pretty good-size—"

"They left Dorene Coe in Trinity Park," I said. "So I thought we could look there first. If she's not there then we can go look in all those little streets and alleys around the Will Rogers area."

"And if she's not there either?"

"Then we go home."

"There's got to be a catch to it," Harry said. "Anyway, aren't patrol cars already looking in all of those places?"

"Of course," I said, "but the pickup truck—"

"Is up higher so you can see more. Right," Harry said. Then he shrugged. "On one condition."

"Which is?"

"If we don't find her you buy me ice cream on the way home."

That sounded fair enough to me.

Cameron would not want to be fed again until about ten and anyway he had me along, but just in case I got busy I put a bottle in the diaper bag. I mean I put a bottle of water in the diaper bag and I put in a plastic bag containing the little scoops of powder that mix up with the water to make formula. I saw to it there were plenty of diapers. I got two Cokes out of the refrigerator, a Coke with sugar and caffeine for Harry, and a caffeine-free Diet Coke for me, and then we took off.

It was really a nice evening for a drive. It had cooled off just enough to be pleasant but not enough to be chilly, and it was nice and clear and every now and then, when we were far enough away from the streetlights, we could see that the stars were out although the sky was still more a deep blue than real black. I had strapped Cameron, per state law, securely into a safety seat between Harry and me, and fastened my own seat belt and maneuvered myself into a position such that I could put my feet on the dash, which Harry says is an abominable habit, but I maintain that if he were my height he'd do it too when he wasn't driving.

Trinity Park. Trees and the river and people feeding ducks and people jogging and people embracing on the lawn under trees. I didn't look too closely at them—only closely enough to be sure they were alive. Not that I particularly suspected our robbers of necrophilia, but after the way they had fooled those two teenagers—

There aren't really that many little roads in Trinity Park. There are some. But only some. We drove around to all the zoo parking, some of which gets rather deserted-looking at some times of night.

If Deandra Black was anywhere near Trinity Park, we didn't find her.

"Stockyards next?" Harry said.

"Well, not exactly the stockyards." The old stockyards

are down by the now-defunct Billy Bob's, which once was the largest bar in Texas (I mean, how many bars do *you* know that are big enough to have rodeos inside them?). The Fat Stock Show area is not the stockyards area.

I explained the area I had in mind, and Harry said, "You got it."

There is a sort of wedge-shape chunk of land, intersected by many streets, which includes the Fat Stock Show area (consider it a fairgrounds—the Fat Stock Show is Fort Worth's answer to the Texas State Fair in Dallas)—and also a lot of museums that don't to most people's minds have much to do with the Fat Stock Show. There are a lot of buildings. A lot of corrals and display barns and little alleyways and roads and parking lots and so forth. We did a surprisingly large amount of driving for the size—on paper—of the space.

I had a good flashlight, and I was using it. There were so many dark areas. Under trees—a lot of trees. Behind and beside and between loading docks. Inside barns.

A patrol car came along once and stopped us and the patrol officer asked us what we thought we were doing. I showed my identification and told him what we thought we were doing, and he said, "Good luck. I already checked it all."

But he hadn't—quite—checked it all.

Because I found her.

At first I thought it was a dog or something.

Then I thought it was a street person who had crawled up on a grassy bank on the far side of a loading dock to sleep. It would have been a pretty good place to sleep, and she was wrapped in a blanket.

But I thought I would get out of the car to check, just to be sure.

"Deb, be careful," Harry said tensely.

"I'm being careful." As I walked up the bank I was aware that Harry had his own pistol—he has a permit to carry it—in his hand. He was more scared than I was, because he is less used to this type of situation. I wasn't scared. Just cautious. Just cautious.

It wasn't until I was actually up the bank standing beside her that I knew for sure who it was. Even then I wasn't a hundred percent sure. Her face seemed drained of blood. But her eyes were shut. Her eyes were shut. Corpses' eyes aren't shut, not until somebody shuts them.

But she couldn't be alive. Not with the gaping hole and the blood on the olive-drab army blanket, the gaping hole in her torso, she couldn't be alive. But her chest rose and fell once. Her hand moved—

I know first aid. But not for that severe a wound. "Harry!" I shouted. "Turn on your radio!"

We cannot afford—nor would either one of us want—a car telephone. But Harry has put CB radios in both my car and his truck, and also a ham—shortwave—radio in the truck.

"Send for an ambulance!"

He didn't ask why. He just got on channel 9, the emergency channel, and after a while that was probably not as long a while as it seemed to me, crouching beside a critically injured, unconscious—but living—woman, somebody from REACT answered, and a moment later—not much of a moment, because the closest fire station was fairly near—I could hear sirens in the air.

Sirens, not siren, because Fort Worth has the quaint custom of dispatching a fire truck on every ambulance call. I did not, and do not, and never shall, understand the reason for that.

And more sirens, because police units—beginning, of course, with the patrolman who thought he had checked the area thoroughly—were coming too.

"How did you think to look for her here?" Millner asked.

"I just had a feeling," I said meekly.

"Remind me not to yell about your hunches again," Millner said.

He would, of course. And quite rightly. Because about one-third of my hunches were valid and the other two-thirds were a complete waste. Of course Millner knew just as well as I did that the one-third when they were accurate were well worth the wasted time when they weren't, but that didn't alter the fact that the time would be wasted and I would feel guilty and Millner would yell.

Dorene Coe had been shot in the head with a pistol. Deandra Black had been shot in the torso with a shotgun. Could we surmise different people were doing the shooting?

Maybe the one Carlos hit was the one who shot Dorene? So now the other one had been the one who shot Deandra?

Every gunshot wound reported in the metroplex area had been checked by police in the jurisdiction where it was reported. Every reported gunshot victim in the metroplex area had been cleared of involvement in this particular case.

Somewhere in the metroplex there was somebody—probably, but not certainly, a man, because few women use guns that big—with an inadequately treated wound. If he didn't get to a doctor soon, the law wouldn't need to deal with him. Nature would deal with him, quite adequately.

Leaving Sarah working, Harry and I went home. I put Cameron to bed and called Susan.

That is Dr. Susan Braun. Psychiatrist. Owner-director of one of Fort Worth's finest private psychiatric hospitals.

Most people I would hesitate to call after nine o'clock at night. But not Susan. A night owl from way back, she expressed delight at hearing from me and at once announced she had just made a cake and was going to come over and share it with me. She hung up before I had time to say I didn't want any cake. You don't suppose I'm trying to get anorexic, do you?

Surely not.

"I'm going to go read in bed," Harry said. "Tell Susan hi for me. And remember you have to get up in the morning."

The best that I can figure out, it was during the time that I was picking up the living room a little and sticking the dishes into the dishwasher, during the time that Susan was driving from her clinic where she lives as well as works, that Vic Gardner's house went up in flames.

I didn't know about that until a whole lot later.

It wasn't in Fort Worth, you see. It was in a little community north of Keller, going in the direction of Denton. The volunteer firemen there knew they had a problem, because Vic Gardner's house contained his office, and his front yard and side yard and backyard contained a whole lot of scrap automobiles. They knew they had a potentially big fire and they asked for help from Keller and Keller asked for help from Fort Worth.

They had a hunch Vic Gardner was inside the house, because his wrecker was parked in the yard, and Vic drank pretty heavily and smoked a lot and they figured that was probably what had started the fire. But by the time they got there, there wasn't the ghost of a hope of getting him out alive.

It wasn't until the next day, when they found Vic's body, that they knew he'd been shot.

And it wasn't until I got there, a lot later the next day, that anybody began to have an idea why.

· 8 ·

"You think he hates women," I repeated, stirring at my now-somewhat-cool hot chocolate.

Susan removed the bobby pins from her left braid and began to unbraid. "He or they," she emphasized. "I mean, who did what? Who does what? Who's giving the orders? You don't know that and neither do I. But at least one of them hates women. The one who shot Dorene Coe might not. He might just—I don't know how to put it. He might just think he's efficient. You kill the witness that could identify you. But—the one that shot Deandra Black—Deb, he knew he hadn't killed her. From what you tell me, he had to know. And he just walked off and left her to die alone in the dark. That's not efficiency. That's hatred."

I picked up the little paper saucer I'd served my piece of cake on—half the piece was still on it—and reached for Susan's. A sliver of cake remained on it too. "I'm through," she said, randomly inserting bobby pins in the general vicinity of the remodeled braid. "But I wish you'd eat the rest of yours."

"Why does everybody keep trying to feed me?" I asked. When I asked Harry, earlier in the day, it was a rhetorical question. But Susan might really know. Susan seems to know a lot of things.

"Because you look half starved," she answered. "Deb, you are at least thirty pounds thinner than you were last September."

"Last September I was pregnant."

"Last September—when the month started—you were eight weeks pregnant. You weren't showing. If anything you were losing a little weight, because you weren't eating anything and if you did you barfed it. You gained too much weight the last three months, but you've lost it all and then some."

"I needed to lose a little weight."

"A little. Not thirty pounds. Deb, what do you weigh right now?"

"I don't know," I mumbled.

"Then you have a pretty good idea. What did you weigh at your six-week checkup?"

"Ninety-eight pounds," I said, striving for inaudibility.

"You ought to weigh a hundred and twenty."

"You're a shrink, not a dietician."

"I'm a physician before I'm a shrink. I know when somebody's underweight. You ought to weigh a hundred and twenty pounds and you know it. No wonder everybody's trying to feed you. You look like it wouldn't even take a strong wind to blow you away."

"I don't want to talk about my weight. I want to talk about—"

"About the bank robbers. I know. I've given you all I can think of. I ought to leave and let you go to sleep."

"It won't do any good. I've got to feed Cameron in half an hour. He should have already woken up."

"Go wake him up."

"But—"

"Deb, you are supposed to train the baby. He is not supposed to train you. What's he doing right now, sleeping through his ten o'clock feeding and waking for the two A.M.?"

"That's exactly what he's doing. How did you guess?"

"By how tired you are. Go wake him up and feed him. Keep waking him up if he tries to go to sleep. Then when he tries to wake up at two A.M. ignore him."

I grimaced. "That's like ignoring a tornado siren."

"Ignore him anyway." Then she shrugged. "Well, if you can't you can't. But start waking him up about nine and deliberately keeping him awake awhile and then feeding him and putting him down. It might help."

So I woke Cameron up and fed him and at 2 A.M. he woke up and I tried, not very successfully and not very long—maybe about five minutes or so—to ignore him, and then I got up and fed him and of course I felt half dead when I had to get up at six to feed him again and there was no use at all trying to go back to sleep because Hal had left in the pickup truck to go to seminary—that's an early-morning religion class he goes to five days a week, in common with almost all Mormon teenagers—and by the time I could go back to sleep Hal would be banging back in telling me many things I did not want to know, all about church history, which is what he is studying this year, and by the time he settled down it would be time for me to leave anyway. So obviously I was up for the day.

I changed Cameron and fed him and bathed him—I know Harry could do that but I like to—and gave Harry and Hal ham and cheese omelets for breakfast. I had a bowl of Special K myself, which I think is not exactly what Susan would prescribe for my breakfast right now unless I accompanied it with a large bowl of ice cream—and then I left for work, hoping to get there a little early so I could catch up on reports. I was, the best I could figure out, about two days behind, and Captain Millner was likely to be screaming at me pretty soon if I didn't do something about this matter.

When I got in I didn't start on reports immediately. Instead I called the hospital Deandra Black had been taken to. She was alive. She was in critical condition. No, she was not conscious and if she were conscious she certainly would not be up to talking with police and I should have better sense than to ask such a silly question.

So I dictated reports onto tapes and I was still doing that at nine o'clock, when Captain Millner came into the office. "What are you doing?" he asked me.

"Making reports. What does it look like I'm doing?"

"You want to go to Keller? Or rather, north of Keller?"

"What do I want to go north of Keller for?" I asked warily.

I live in northeast Tarrant County, outside of the city limits of anything, although I'm sure that sooner or later the city of Fort Worth will annex us. Southeast of where I live, which is called Summerfields Addition, is a very small town called Keller. Hal goes to school at Keller High School, in a very nice new building that was worth an increase in my school taxes. North—or at least sort of north—of Keller is Denton Highway, which is the highway you take to get to Denton, which is where Texas Woman's University and North Texas University live. Between Keller and Denton are several small towns, one of which is very cute. There is a highway speed limit sign—fifty-five miles per hour. About ten feet past it is a city limits sign to a town that shall remain nameless here because I don't want to advertise it. About five feet past that sign is a speed limit sign. This one says fifteen miles per hour. Or at least it did last time I looked. Need I say that I avoid driving through that town?

"You know anything about a Gardner's Wrecking Yard?"

"I've passed it." Actually I had had more contact than that with it. It was Gardner's that had hauled away my Lynx about two months ago, when it became evident it was no longer going anywhere under its own power.

"It burned last night."

"Oh? The whole wrecking yard?"

"Gardner's house and office. What's to burn in the rest of a wrecking yard?"

"What are you telling me this for?" I inquired.

"I told you, I want you to go out there."

"Why? It's not our jurisdiction and—"

Need I say I was a little slow that morning?

"Because," Millner said, sounding somewhat irritated, "the fire marshal managed to get in there this morning. They found Vic Gardner, or rather what was left of him—at least they assume it's Gardner, because it's a little hard to be sure—on what was left of his couch, which was a little less than what was left of him. And they found a whole bunch of shotgun pellets in Gardner's chest and belly and in and around the couch."

"Oh, shit," I said.

"It's on Denton Highway," Millner added. "Bob's en route from ident."

I went by my house, which was only about three blocks out of the way, to get the boots I usually wear to arsons. They are not normal women's boots, which are designed to look pretty; rather, they are boots designed for teenage boys. I figured if they would hold up to teenage boys they would hold up to arsons. So far I have been right, and I have been wearing them for three years, a few times into boiling water. If the fire was last night, I would not be wading through boiling water this time. But I would be wading through water, and probably chemicals, and ashes, and a lot of crud. Definitely this was a job for the fire boots.

Some years ago Lady Bird Johnson, who at that time was residing in Washington, D.C., got this wonderful idea that wrecking yards are ugly. Nobody else had ever noticed that. Lady Bird had another idea—they should be concealed from the street by nice board or plastic lathing fences, and it would be nice to plant morning glories or rambler roses or something nice like that on the fences.

Surprisingly, a lot of state legislatures passed laws dictating that should be done.

Even more surprisingly, some wrecking yard owners in states that hadn't passed such laws put up fences and planted rambler roses and morning glories.

Vic Gardner did not put up a fence. That is, he did not put up an opaque fence; he did of course have a ten-foot-high hurricane fence with barbed wire on top so that nobody could steal car parts from him without getting holes in the seats of their pants.

Vic Gardner did not plant rambler roses or morning glories on his fence.

Vic Gardner had one of the ugliest wrecking yards I have ever seen, and no wrecking yard is what you would call beautiful. He apparently did not believe in selling cars to those places that crunch cars up and sell them to steel mills; no, he apparently assumed that sooner or later there would be a use for every part on every car he hauled in. So there were cars—or rusting hulls of cars—twenty and thirty years old at the back of the lot. His front porch was tastefully festooned with about six million hubcaps of all sizes and shapes, and a hand-lettered sign partially obscured by several of the hubcaps announced, unnecessarily in my opinion, that he had car parts for sale.

In his front yard was a reasonable, or maybe unreasonable, imitation suit of armor made entirely of car parts. Maybe it was meant to be Don Quixote or Sancho Panza instead of a suit of armor. Or maybe it was meant to be somebody from outer space. Or Atlantis. I couldn't exactly tell.

In his wrecking yard were fourteen, count 'em, fourteen blue Mercury Lynxes of various ages and conditions.

This did not bespeak great intelligence on the part of the killers. I mean, what was the sense in killing Vic Gardner and burning his house around him, when all we had to do was go check the VINs—vehicle identification numbers—and run the cars for registration?

So thought I.

Until I got closer and found that smilax and kudzu were growing around every one of those cars. None of those cars was the one that had been hauled in last Saturday from in front of a day-care center.

One of them, in fact, as I should have realized, was my own late unlamented vehicle.

In that case, why the killing? Why the fire? Millner had sent me out here assuming a relationship between this killing and fire and our bank robberies, and I had come out here with the same thing in mind, but if there wasn't a relationship—

If there wasn't a relationship then this whole thing made no sense at all whatever. There had to be a relationship.

Leaving Bob taking pictures, I continued to prowl around the wrecking yard. There had to be a connection. There had to be a reason.

A lot of tire tracks, from a lot of fire trucks and police cars. And there, in one corner of the wrecking yard proper as distinguished from the yard of the house—which contained only the choicer and possibly restorable pieces of vehicle—a set of tire tracks away from the others.

Actually two sets of tire tracks, largely but not totally superimposed one on the other. The first set had dug in deep, especially the rear wheels. The second was a lighter vehicle, or less loaded down, or both.

Marks in what would have been midaxle, as if a chain or rope had hit the ground hard. A few footprints.

The second car, the lighter one, had been towed.

I went to get Bob.

Photographs, using a special camera on a special rack that allows the camera to point straight down and forces the picture, when it is blown up to standard 8 × 10 format, to be exactly life-size.

Then plaster casts. You mix the plaster with water. You spray something like hair spray into the footprint or tire track so that it won't be damaged by the plaster. Then you pour the plaster in, very carefully, using the stirring spatula to break the force of the flow so that, again, you won't damage what you're trying to preserve. You put in some sticks and twigs to strengthen the cast and then you pour in more plaster and then you wait until it's completely hard and then you lift it intact, without trying to clean the dirt off it because the lab would prefer to do that itself, and then you put it in a cardboard box if it's small enough or on a plank or something if it's too large for a cardboard box, and then you take it in.

With luck, you find a tire or a shoe to match the cast before the tire or shoe has worn enough more that the match is no longer evident.

If you can catch it soon enough it's almost as good as fingerprints.

This was not anything that would lead us to the killers. There are too many of any kind of tire, too many of any kind of shoe. But once we caught them another way—if we caught them soon enough—this would be another piece of evidence to help convict them.

There was no use for me to stand around and wait while the casts hardened, a process that can take an hour or two if the plaster is in a nasty mood, and don't tell me plaster is inanimate and cannot get in a nasty mood. I know that. But when you're working with it you don't believe that for a second. Sometimes it is perfectly cooperative and other times it is beastly. Sometimes it hardens into what can only be called a plaster disaster, solidifying in the bucket before you have time to pour it, and other times you spend three hours waiting while it sits there in a dispirited puddle. There is probably some wonderful scientific reason relating to atmospheric conditions why it does those awful things, but I don't know what it is.

And since I'm no longer in ident I don't need to know.

I walked back to the house and asked the fire marshal, a fellow by the name of Rich Owings, whether any of the wrecking yard's records had been salvaged.

Rich, who was talking with Neal Ryan from the Rangers, paused long enough to grimace at me. "Are you kidding?" he asked. "That looked like where the accelerant was poured."

It would have been, of course.

But suppose—just suppose—

When my car became inoperable and Vic Gardner paid me a hundred dollars cash for the dubious privilege of hauling it off, he gave me the hundred literally in cash and I signed the title over to him. He said he'd get it notarized later, which is probably not quite legal, but I didn't feel it made much difference when the car was being junked anyway.

He took the cash out of his pocket and he put the title in his pocket.

But he also made some notes on a clipboard on the seat of his wrecker.

The wrecker hadn't been burned; it was sitting in the front yard underneath a live oak tree, the doors unlocked. If my blond Harrison Ford fan hadn't remembered that clipboard—

She hadn't. Because there it was.

With a certain feeling of triumph, I reached for it.

And then paused. Did I need a search warrant for this? The laws now state you have to have a search warrant to search a crime scene. Well, actually, it wasn't the laws that said that, it was the courts.

Certainly somebody had gotten a warrant to search this as the scene of an arson. But the laws regarding search warrants are very, very funny. I'll try to explain.

You are allowed to look in any place the thing you are looking for might reasonably be concealed, and if you find something else illegal there then you may legally seize it. Thus the police and Secret Service agents who served a search warrant to look for the press that was printing counterfeit money, and were astonished to find a crank laboratory—that is, an underground methamphetamine laboratory—in the basement, were legal. The printing press *could* have been in the basement. But if they had been serving a search warrant to look for a stolen car and had found the crank lab in the basement, they could not—then or ever—make a case on the crank lab. Because the stolen car could not be in the basement. So they had no business being in the basement either.

What this meant right now was that if Rich Owings had taken a search warrant to look for the cause of a fire that was suspected to be arson, his finding shotgun pellets in and around Vic Gardner was legal, because the accelerant could have been dumped on the couch Vic Gardner was lying on.

But if that was the search warrant under which we were still working now, then I was illegal.

The fire didn't start in the truck. The fire didn't ever get to the truck.

No, Bob wasn't illegal, because those footprints, those tire tracks, very probably were related to the arson.

I decided I had better find out what search warrant we were working under and what it specified. I went and asked.

Neal grinned at me. "I wish everybody was as careful as

you are," he said. "It's my warrant. I got it after Rich called me this morning. We're searching for anything that might provide a motive to the killing. And I specified outbuildings and vehicles."

I went back and got the dirty metal clipboard and started looking through the papers stacked haphazardly on it.

It wasn't very far down.

No, of course the title wasn't there. Unless Gardner had already filed it and I didn't expect he had—he had ten days to do it in and from what I knew of him I doubted he would do anything until the last minute—the title was gone, burned along with everything in Gardner's pockets and on his desk.

But there was a piece of paper on which he had scrawled "Blue Lynx with hood up." And the name of a day-care center with an address in Keller.

Hallelujah.

Except that this presented another problem.

Right now, presumably, the day-care center was safe, because they—the perpetrators, to use a nice chunk of jargon—thought all records we could use to trace that Lynx had burned. If they found out otherwise, then the day-care center, and its owner and its workers, and, presumably, the children, were all at risk. Oh, sure, we could keep it out of the papers, off the radio and television.

But kids talk.

Kids talk.

We didn't know what age this kid was, the child the Harrison Ford fan said she had been on her way to pick up when her car conked out. If the kid was a baby then he—or she—couldn't talk. But we couldn't assume that. If he was a three-year-old, a four-year-old, and Mama went to pick him up and he started talking about police showing up at the center—well, she'd know why.

Or at least she'd guess why.

We couldn't risk that but we had to have the information.

There had to be a way—

There was a way. Of course there was a way.

I told Neal what I was going to do and he didn't just grin, he laughed out loud. Then I went home and called Millner. He thought it was pretty smart too, but reminded me I was in somebody else's jurisdiction and there were professional courtesies involved. I said I knew that, and I called the Keller chief of police.

Then I dressed Cameron in his cutest playsuit, packed the bottle he had reluctantly decided to accept, left the detective car parked in the driveway while I borrowed Harry's pickup truck, strapped Cameron into his car seat, and headed back to Keller.

There are advantages to being female. I'm not saying a man couldn't pull it off, but I'm not a bit sure a man would have thought it up.

The day-care center was a converted house, 1950s tract housing vintage, with dull-green asbestos siding, but the sign in front was cheerfully arrayed with painted lambs and large and improbably colored flowers. When I went in the door, the first worker I saw—a sturdy and cheerful-looking girl of about nineteen—eyed Cameron and said, "Oh, dear, we don't usually take them that small. He's not three months yet, is he?"

"Could I talk with the manager?" I asked, trying to put a slight quaver in my voice and fearing that it sounded more like a whine.

"I really don't think she could make any exceptions—"

"Well, if I could just talk to her—"

"She's busy—"

"I just want to talk to her."

The interchange went on that way for a few more seconds, before the teenager apparently decided I was not going to budge in the slightest degree and went away. She returned a moment later in the wake of a large, white-haired woman, and I could hear her saying "Just won't listen to me—"

"I'll take care of it," the woman said in a cheerfully booming voice. "Now, I'm Phyllis Farmer. What seems to be the problem?"

"If I could just talk with you alone—"

"Oh, dear. Didn't Natalie tell you we don't usually take babies under three months—"

"Yes, but if I could just talk with you alone—" This time I managed to sound as if I were just about to burst into tears.

"Oh, dear," she said again. "Why don't we just step out into the front yard?" As the door shut behind her, she said, "Dear, I know there are financial reasons why some women have to return to work almost immediately, but it would really be better for you and your baby—"

"Truer words were never spoken," I said, "but I don't need to leave my baby here." By now I had my badge case out and open. "I'm Debra Ralston, Fort Worth Police Department, and I need to talk to you—"

Her voice chilling noticeably, she demanded, "And where did you borrow the baby?"

"I didn't. He's my baby. I just don't need to leave him here. My husband is—is sort of a semi-invalid right now. He can't work. So I have to. But he is able to watch the baby."

"Then I don't understand—"

"Mrs. Farmer," I said, "we have reason to believe that you, and your workers, and the children may be in danger."

"What?"

"You are probably aware that there have been two bank robberies recently in which tellers have been kidnapped. One was killed, and one is in serious condition. It appears that the robbers have also, thus far, killed a police officer, the owner of a used car lot, and the owner of a wrecking yard in the effort to protect their identity."

"What does that have to do with—"

"Last Saturday," I said, "a woman left a child here. We don't know what age child. The woman is a blond, about thirty-five. When she came to pick the child up, her car—a blue Mercury Lynx—broke down and had to be towed away. There is a strong probability that woman is involved with the killings. So we need to know who she is."

"Oh, dear," Mrs. Farmer said. "Now that does present a problem."

"Which is?"

She gestured toward the sign. "Of course we have our regulars, children who are here every day. But we also take drop-ins. Yes, I remember the incident, the more so because the mother seemed extremely nervous while she was waiting for her ride and for a tow truck. But the child—a boy, about four—was a drop-in. Not a regular. So I won't be of much use to you—"

"Don't you get information about drop-ins?"

"Oh, yes, but—"

"Can you give me what information you do have?"

"Let's go to my office—"

"Mrs. Farmer," I said, "I don't want there to be any possibility whatever that any of the children know, or even guess, that there was a police officer here today. That's for your protection. So I'm not going into your office. I would suggest you tell your staff that I wouldn't take no for an answer and you went in, checked for openings, and then went back to tell me again that you couldn't help me."

"Mrs.— What did you say your name is again?"

"Ralston. Deb Ralston."

"Mrs. Ralston, do you really think my children are in danger?"

"Not if we can keep the criminals from having any idea at all that we're on the right trail."

"All right. If you really think—"

She went after the information.

It didn't help much.

The child's first name was Scott.

The mother was Kelly McGillis.

Witness. The actress who played the Amish woman whose son saw a gangland killing in a Philadelphia rest room.

Apparently I really was going to have to get a list of all the women who had ever costarred with Harrison Ford.

I could really do without this.

I asked, without much hope, whether Mrs. Farmer had noticed the vehicle or the person who had picked "Kelly McGillis" and her son Scott up after the wrecker removed the Lynx. I might as well not have asked. She had been busy with a two-year-old who had suddenly begun vomiting. And no, none of her workers could have noticed because Saturday is usually a slow day and she didn't have any workers there. She was by herself. Actually it was all right because there were only four children including Scott, but right then, with a sick two-year-old—

I have coped with sick two-year-olds myself. I thanked her and left.

When I deposited Cameron in his playpen the cat came over at once and sat in the playpen twitching his tail just out of reach. Yes, I know that's how cats play with their kittens. But Cameron is not the cat's kitten. Cameron is my kitten, and when he began to howl I evicted the cat. With a very offended look, she climbed up the mesquite tree, sat on a low branch, and dangled her tail for Pat.

Cameron, Pat, I know exactly how you feel. I should name the cat Melanie Griffith Carrie Fisher Kelly McGillis. But she's been a nameless cat ten years. Why should I confuse her by giving her a name now?

By the time I got back in Cameron had apparently forgotten all about the cat and was trying to eat his Cradle Gym, though his frequent glances at the blank television screen suggested he was hoping Harry and I would begin to play Nintendo.

Ha. I have never played a video game yet. Why should I begin now?

I asked Harry if he wanted a cheese sandwich. He seemed to be busily filling out some kind of forms and told me he did not want a cheese sandwich.

Fine. I made myself a cheese sandwich. After eating it, I called Captain Millner and told him the results of that attempt at investigation, and then I left in the police car to go talk to a few people.

I wasn't—yet—quite prepared to give up on Nick Casavetes. Not until after I had talked with Lonzo Hambly and Rita Cleveland.

9

Rita Cleveland was pretty if you like that type. This is about as close to an unprejudiced statement about her as I can make, because frankly I disliked her on sight. Her hair probably had started out blond, but somewhere on the way it had been frosted, bleached, curling-ironed, teased, and otherwise manipulated out of all recognition. Literally. It looked about as much like feathers—wet feathers that had dried stuck together—as it did like human hair. In front the bangs—I don't know what else to call them—stuck out about four inches in front of her face; she must have used as much gel as Tammy Faye Bakker uses makeup to get them to stay in that position. Her light-blue chambray shirt was open at the top four buttons, and her denim skirt was about four inches long. Her high-heel sandals were about six inches high and her baby was about six months old.

Nick Casavetes hadn't mentioned the baby. I wondered whether it was his.

She had so much goop on her face I would have been afraid it would crack her face to talk except that she was chewing gum—about four pieces of it—with her mouth open. She stopped chewing long enough to tell me, in a Marilyn Monroe–style voice, that yes she was Rita Cleveland and ask why I wanted to know.

I showed my identification and she instantly looked scared, which was interesting, because although some people are always scared of the police that tends to be a cultural thing, and despite her own appearance Rita Cleveland lived in a nice brick house in a nice suburb of Bedford, which in general is a nice bedroom community. There were nice—nicey-nice—furnishings in the house, which didn't look like the kind of house where a person who was always afraid of the police would live.

But that is a stereotype. I remember one night I got a call to a suicide—that was when I was still in ident—and I went to about a half-million-dollar house in a very, very nice neighborhood indeed. The husband of the victim, seeing my camera and thinking I was a reporter, had to be physically restrained by three uniform officers from attacking me. The victim was tarted up worse than Rita Cleveland. There was no question about it being suicide; we had to break down the locked and bolted door of her bedroom to get in, and when we did we found her hand was clutching the revolver in that cadaveric spasm that happens only with absolutely instant death, and it took three of us to pry it loose. Her son, about seventeen, was hysterical in the living room. In the kitchen a pan of chocolate chip cookies was on top of the stove. Half of the cookies had been lifted off with a spatula and put on newspapers on the kitchen table; the other half were now almost cemented to the pan.

I wondered why she had shot herself. Devoted husband, devoted son, evidence of domestic activity—

In the emergency room, where she was examined before being moved to the morgue, a compassionate nurse moved by heaven only knows what impulse washed the woman's face—and her hair fell off. That frosted bouffant five-years-outdated coiffure was a wig. Under it she had pleasant light-brown hair, neatly combed. And beneath the almost grotesque makeup was a good complexion, a little pale, sprinkled with tiny freckles. She was pretty, without the makeup, without the wig.

I still hadn't heard her name. And when I did I still didn't quite understand, until one of the men on the intelligence unit explained to me. Her husband was a small-time mafioso who had been kicked out of the mafia.

He ran a string of prostitutes.

When he had more business than they could handle he turned his wife on the street.

This time she had refused to go. Refused in the only way she could make stick.

But a mafioso's daughter wouldn't be hanging around with a punk like Nick Casavetes. No, most likely this girl was the heartache of the decent, respectable parents who had bought and furnished this decent, respectable house, had paid for the braces and other dental work that gave Rita her perfect, straight, white teeth, had bought the sober, respectable Dodge K car I'd seen in the front of the house.

What was funny in a sad sort of way was that Rita was probably really a perfectly decent girl herself, and she'd come to realize it sometime in the next five to ten years. It could be hoped that she wouldn't damage herself irreparably before that time.

"What do you want?" she demanded, dangling the baby in a way that made me want to snatch him to safety.

An older woman walked into the room, glanced anxiously at the baby, and then looked at me.

"I'm Deb Ralston," I said again. "Fort Worth Police Department."

And there was the fear in her eyes. But hers was understandable, especially when she turned to the girl and said, "Rita, is there something you haven't told me?"

"Uh-uh," Rita said, chewing emphatically. "I don't know what she wants."

"Rita hasn't done anything," I said quickly. "I just want to ask a few questions about Nick Casavetes."

"My daughter isn't seeing him anymore," the woman—Mrs. Cleveland?—said quickly.

Maybe she believed that, although I doubted it. I certainly didn't. I'd seen the quick flash in Rita's eyes. She might or might not have been with Nick Casavetes Saturday morning, but she certainly was still seeing him.

"That's fine, then she won't mind answering some questions about him," I said heartily. "Rita, would you mind coming out to the car with me? There's something I want to show you."

There wasn't, especially, but I wanted to get her out of earshot of her mother. You'd think she would have appreciated that, but instead she said, "You can call me Miss Cleveland."

"Oh, Rita!" the older woman said, her tone more resigned than anything else.

"You're quite right," I agreed. "I should call you Miss Cleveland. I just wasn't thinking. You don't mind coming out to the car with me, do you?"

She shrugged, smacked her gum in a manner carefully calculated to annoy any adult present, and sort of tossed the baby to her mother. "I guess not."

Outside, in the front yard, I said, "I don't really have anything to show you. I just wanted to talk with you outside."

"I figured that. Mom's a nosy old broad."

"I wouldn't know about that, but I did want to respect your privacy." What I really wanted to do was spank her, but of course that was out of the question. "Did you see Nick Saturday morning?"

"Oh, yeah."

"What time?"

"Oh, I don't know, I wasn't paying no attention to the time. Maybe it was ten, maybe it was eleven. I don't know." The deliberately slovenly grammar could not—quite—conceal upper-middle-class diction.

"What did he do when he got here?"

"He didn't come in. You think *she'd* let Nick in? Of course. I was watching for him from my bedroom window. Then I told Mom I was going to the lake with some girlfriends and I went on out. He had the boat and we went up to Lake Dallas."

"How long did you stay there?"

"All day."

"Until dark?"

"I mean all day. He brought me home about midnight."

"About midnight."

"Yeah. Mom and Dad were already asleep."

"Was your baby asleep?"

"I don't know."

"You don't know?"

"Uh-uh. He sleeps in Mom's room."

I didn't have any more questions. Unless Rita was lying—and as much as I would like to believe that I had no reason to—Nick Casavetes had been with her part of Saturday morning.

The problem was that she didn't know what part of Saturday morning. That said—or at least suggested—that he didn't need an alibi. Because if he needed an alibi he'd see to it she knew what time he'd arrived even if he had to lie about it and convince her to believe the lie.

Or else he'd have her lying for him.

I didn't think Rita Cleveland was lying.

I thanked her and watched her slouch back into the house, swinging her hips every inch of the way.

Next stop, Presto Boats in Euless.

Which I could not find.

I knew it was situated somewhere in a block of warehouses, and I had the address of the block of warehouses. I drove straight to it, with no trouble at all. Presto was supposed to be number E-4 and I drove back and forth and up and down and around and around and could not find E-4. Finally I stopped and asked, but the person I asked had no idea where building E was and had never heard of Presto Boats so I asked someone else who was in the same situation and then, oh frabjous day, I found a mail carrier.

It seemed that buildings B, D, F, and G were where I was. Buildings A, C, E, and G were across the freeway. The phone book showed them all at the same address because the office was in building B.

Across the freeway. That meant I had to find the exit I came in on and drive across—not back onto the freeway, but under it. But then I found out I couldn't get to it that way because I would have been going the wrong way on a one-way frontage road, so I got back out onto the freeway (a chore that involved making a U-turn in the middle of a very crowded parking lot) and drove up the freeway to the *next* exit and exited and came back down the frontage road, going the right way this time, and found Presto Boats with no trouble at all. It had only taken me half an hour.

Once located it was fairly, unmistakable. Boats—mostly larger boats than you would expect to find in inland Texas unless you'd seen some of the monster yachts that inhabit Lake Dallas—were standing about in the yard and parking lot in various stages of completion. These weren't cheap speedboats or flat-bottomed fishing rigs. These were big boats, a few outboards but mostly inboards, trimmed with brass and cedar and mahogany. The casual-sounding name "Presto Boats" was misleading. Lonzo Hambly catered to the carriage trade.

Nick Casavetes was standing at a power saw wearing goggles and cutting plywood, but that didn't prevent him from looking at me and smirking.

I did not like Nick Casavetes.

I especially did not like the fact that if he'd been shot recently he certainly couldn't have been moving as freely as he was. Though of course it could have been the other one who was hit.

The sound of power equipment was deafening. I wondered whether I ought to try to ask somebody where Lonzo Hambly was, or just wander around and look lost until he came and found me. I was spared the decision when a young woman—definitely not our Harrison Ford fan, she was about twenty-three and had black hair—asked me, loudly and rather hoarsely, if she could help me find something. I shouted, "I need to talk to Lonzo Hambly."

"This way," she yelled, and led me to a small office. She knocked—how she expected anybody to hear over the noise is absolutely beyond me—and then opened the door and said, "Lonzo, this lady wants to see you."

I stepped into an immensely bright room, closed the door, and turned my head in time to see a sheet of paper held about two inches from somebody's eyes. He put the paper down on the desk and on top of it he put the huge magnifying glass he'd had between his eyes and the paper. As the door shut, the noise dropped by about ninety-five percent, as the old man's face turned toward me. His face. Not his eyes, which were both almost completely covered by dead-white cataracts.

Lonzo Hambly had told me over the telephone that Nick Casavetes had clocked in at five minutes till ten. But Lonzo Hambly literally couldn't see two inches in front of his face.

"Well? What are you waiting for?" he demanded testily. "You wanted to see Lonzo Hambly. You're looking at him."

"I'm Deb Ralston," I said. "I talked with you over the phone yesterday—"

"About that worthless no-good Nick Casavetes. I remember. Not a bit like his brother—"

"Oh, he's got a brother?"

"Didn't I just say so?"

Could it all be coming together this quickly? Was it Casavetes's brother who had clocked in for him? Or was it his brother who robbed banks after Nick checked them out?

Well, no. Because Hambly was continuing. "Always on time, Phil is. Never misses an hour of work, much less a day. If it wasn't for him I'da fired Nick fourteen times a'ready no matter how good he works when he is working. But trouble is, if I fire him then he goes and sponges offa Phil and that's no good. 'Cause Phil is the best worker I got."

"And that's Phil Casavetes. Nick's brother. Was he here Monday?"

"Of course he was here Monday. Didn't I just say he never misses work?"

"And he was here when Nick clocked in."

"Yes'm he was."

"He couldn't have gotten sorry for Nick and clocked in for him?"

"Miz Ralston, Phil Casavetes has worked for me for ten years and he never clocked in for nobody else before now. So why would he decide to do it on Monday? Besides that wasn't I standing right there? And don't I know the difference between Nick and Phil?"

"Mr. Hambly, if you can't see very well—"

"I can *hear,* now can't I? Course it was Nick clocked in."

"And you're sure of the time."

"When I heard the time clock and then heard Nick running that mouth of his I ast Sandra what time it was and Sandra told me it was five minutes short of ten o'clock."

"That was Sandra who brought me in here?"

"That was Sandra. Now, you got anything else you wanta ast me? 'Cause if you don't I got work to do."

His desk was piled with papers. Mentally shuddering at the thought of having to deal with all that with the aid of a magnifying glass, I thanked him and departed.

It was now two o'clock. If I got into the police station as fast as I could I might—might—have time to make a fourth of the reports I needed to make today.

But before I left I got Sandra to show me Phil Casavetes. She was glad to.

Phil Casavetes was shorter than his brother. Stripped to the waist except for safety goggles, he was planing a piece of lumber that apparently was going to be part of the framework to a boat. There was certainly no indication that he had been shot.

"So where did you spend the afternoon?" Millner asked me in a rather disagreeable tone.

Forebearing to point out that the afternoon was far from over, I replied, "In the HEB area asking questions about Nick Casavetes."

Millner slammed the clipboard in his hand down on the desk hard, and I jumped. "Deb," he said in a carefully controlled voice, "would you please spend some time concentrating on something useful? Please? Just for once, would you leave the wild hares to chase themselves? We've already figured out that Casavetes is clear. You know yourself he could not have gotten from that bank to that boat plant in the time he had available to do it in if he was the perpetrator. Anyway I checked his record and he hasn't got one. Well, no criminal record. Army record. *Good* army record. He was in the Special Forces."

"Special Forces?"

"Green Berets. Does that ring a bell?"

Actually it did. I'd met a Green Beret once. He'd told me about the special training he'd gotten. It included a lot of things. He could get just about anywhere and do just about anything without getting caught. One of the things he could do was wriggle through the jungle on his stomach and cut a sentry's throat before the sentry could hear anything or have time to yell.

He told me he'd done that seventy-two times. Slipped up and cut a sentry's throat. A Viet Cong sentry each time, he specified, with a look on his face that made me wonder.

When I talked with him he was just out of a three-year sentence in a minimum-security prison, which was not exactly the best place I could think of to put a man who'd been caught smuggling thirty pounds of cocaine in a military transport plane, and somewhat less time than I would want to put him anywhere.

I asked him why he did it.

He told me he didn't much care. Sure he knew cocaine could kill. But, he said, he didn't have much respect for human life left anyway. It bleeds away so fast, so quietly.

Of course I knew he was the rarity. Of course I knew most of the Green Berets were law-abiding citizens, just like most of the people in any army who go home and put the war away when it's over. I had never asked Harry how many people he had killed during that same war and he would never tell me. Could never tell me even if I did ask, because he killed mostly from the air.

Mostly but not entirely.

That military .45 he'd worn during those years was not an ornament.

But if the Green Beret I met was the exception, that didn't mean he was the only exception.

One thing Nick Casavetes certainly would know is that human life bleeds away fast.

Millner was still glaring at me. I sat down at my desk and got out the little tape recorder we use to dictate reports for the secretaries to type later, and I had just turned it on when Millie came in and said, "Robbery in progress, Southwest Federal, Belknap Road branch."

Millner got up and headed for the door. I didn't. Yet. The Southwest Federal Bank branch on Belknap could wait for me. I telephoned the dispatch office and asked a dispatch to call the Euless Police Department and have an officer go by and check to see if Nick Casavetes was at work.

Then I thought some more. I could see no really good

reason why I needed to go to the scene at all. They would be bringing all the witnesses in to be talked with. They would be bringing in the videotape of the crime. What I wanted to do on this investigation I could do just fine—in fact a lot better—sitting right here at my desk.

I got out the telephone book and started calling automobile dealerships.

I was still calling automobile dealerships, and feeling very discouraged, when Millner came back an hour and a half later. "Whatcha doing, Deb?" he demanded.

I told him.

"Did it ever cross your mind that this might be a different set of perpetrators?"

We never used to talk about "perpetrators" in this police department. But there have been so many cop shows on TV that police all across the country are picking up the slang of the New York PD and the LAPD and thinking that's the way all police have to talk. It makes me a little tired sometimes.

"No," I said, "that did not cross my mind." Though of course it was possible. Fort Worth is not the bank robbery capital of the universe, but we do get enough to keep us busy. "Is it a different set?"

"I wish I knew," Millner said. He sat down at Dutch's desk, leaned back, put his feet on the desk, and pulled his hat down over his eyes. "I sure as hell wish I knew. Figure this one out. The other two descriptions have been pretty clear. Two white males. One tall and one short. This time, both average height, neither appreciably taller than the other and neither one anywhere near my height."

Millner is six foot four.

"Then it's different—"

"But," he went on, ignoring my interruption, "both armed with sawed-off shotguns. Teller—woman by the name of Lola Chavez—taken hostage."

"What else?"

"What do you mean, what else? Her car's an eighty-seven Yugo."

"Maybe it'll stall out—"

"We've put lookouts. Of course."

"Of course. Witnesses? Videotapes?"

"Videotapes. Witnesses. Oh, we got a real winner this time. He could have waited ten more minutes—"

The telephone on my desk rang, and I answered it. "On your call to Euless, that's affirmative."

"Affirmative? He was there?"

"That's what they said."

I thought a minute. "Have them go back and see if Phil Casavetes is there."

"Phil Casavetes? I thought you said Nick Casavetes."

"I did. Now I want to know if Phil Casavetes is there too."

"You should have said that to start with. They could have checked them both at the same time."

"I know," I agreed, "but I didn't think of it."

When I hung up Millner was glaring at me. "You never give up, do you, Deb?"

"So I'm a bulldog."

"You know what they call a lady bulldog?" When I stared at him, momentarily rendered speechless, he said hastily, "Never mind. Never mind. I didn't say it."

I shrugged. "What were you saying about witnesses?"

Before he could answer I could hear, in the hall, the chatter of many children's voices, all very excited, and suddenly a Cub Scout—I knew it was a Cub Scout because he was in that cute little blue-and-gold uniform—darted into the major case squad office and back out. What a time for a police department tour, I thought but did not say.

Millner sat up and removed his hat. "The witnesses," he said.

"What?"

"The witnesses," he repeated. "A troop of Cub Scouts was touring the bank. Or a pack. Or whatever. I forget.

You know, there's a big group that's divided into little groups? It was the whole big group—about sixty kids and fifteen adult leaders."

"Cub Scouts—on Wednesday?"

"Teacher work day," Millner said blandly.

"You mean we've got to get statements from sixty Cub Scouts?" I asked feebly.

"You got it, sister."

It could have been worse. They could have taken one of the kids hostage, instead of the teller.

That's what we kept telling ourselves.

Theoretically you do not let the witnesses talk with one another about the crime until after you have gotten statements from all of them. That's not really a workable theory even in the case of adults. In the case of sixty boys ranging in age from eight to almost eleven, well, it's completely and totally and utterly impossible.

I was on about Cub Scout number thirty-one when dispatch called and said a Euless unit had just gotten time to swing by Presto Boats again, and yes, Phil Casavetes was on the job.

Which at this point meant nothing at all. The robbery was two hours ago. And from what I had seen of that place the likelihood that anybody would *really* know where anybody else was two hours ago was just about zip.

Probably Millner was right. I had let my dislike for Casavetes color my perceptions. But damn it, I *knew* he was up to something, and the fact that I didn't know what was driving me nuts. If he wasn't the perpetrator—oh, darn, they had me doing it now—if he wasn't the person who'd pulled the robbery then what *was* he getting away with that he was smirking over our not knowing?

Cub Scouts are very observant. Cub Scouts also are very excitable. Trying to get a nine-year-old to sit still long enough to tell what he saw is the pits. And by now just about every one of the kids had called his parents and we had about seventy or eighty parents roaming around demanding to know whether their kids were going to have to go on the witness stand and asking whether they could take their kids home.

No. Yes. *Please*.

No, we probably aren't going to put sixty Cub Scouts on the witness stand. We probably aren't going to put any Cub Scouts on the witness stand. The adult leaders, yes. The three Eagle Scouts who had been accompanying the Cub Scouts as some sort of leaders-in-training (I'm a little vague about such things, though I'm sure Hal could enlighten me), yes. But not, not, not all sixty Cub Scouts.

The Cubs who had already made statements were sent home with parents, except for the ones whose parents didn't come for them and said they were sure the leaders could get them home, just as they always did from field trips. Those Cubs, and the ones still waiting to give statements, were now having paper airplane races in the hall. That was set up by one of the Eagles, who asked Millie for paper, explained what he was doing, and pointed out that as disruptive as it might be, it wasn't nearly as disruptive as letting the Cubs race each other up and down the hall, as they had been doing previously.

Actually the leaders could get the boys under control. They raised two fingers and each boy who saw that raised two fingers and got quiet and pretty soon every kid was standing around being quiet and holding two fingers in the air.

The problem was that every time the leaders put their hands down again all sixty, or however many boys we had left, started shouting again. Millie was dealing out aspirin wholesale to adults. The Cubs didn't seem to need any.

Millner called a patrolman in and sent him out to K mart with a few dollars. He came back with a whole lot of toy police badges, the kind that come in kids' party kits, and Millner doled them out to the boys, swore them all in as honorary assistant detectives, and told them detectives have to be very, very quiet while they're working.

They were quiet for about seven minutes, which is as long as you can expect kids that age to stay quiet.

I am so glad I don't teach elementary school.

By the time we finally got rid of Cub Scouts, Eagle Scouts, and adult leaders, it was eight o'clock, and I called Harry—of course I had called him earlier to let him know what was going on, but now I wanted to let him know I was going to be on my way home in a minute and what about supper.

Reproachfully, as if I should have guessed, he told me he and Hal had already made supper and it was waiting for me.

Good. I hoped it would keep, because I intended to take Dorene Coe's videotape back. I was surprised Coe hadn't already called us asking about it, because I was sure the store must have been calling him. Though I might have been doing the store an injustice—it was certainly possible that the manager had seen the news, realized what had happened, and decided to write that tape off.

Which they were going to have to do anyway. Videotapes were not made to sit in the sun.

On the front of the brown plastic tape box was a large strip of tape that said "Sounds Easy." I know Sounds Easy—it is a videotape rental chain; I use it often myself.

So I got out the phone book and looked for Sounds Easy locations, trying to find one that was on a straight shot between downtown where Dorene had worked and the northeast Tarrant County area where she had lived (actually, not over five miles from me).

If, like most people, she had gone to the one closest to her house, she had used the same one I use. If she had gone to the one closest to work—well, in that case I'd catch it tomorrow, because I was on my way home now whether anybody liked it or not (and I was fairly sure Captain Millner didn't, in view of the reports I still had not made).

I glanced at my watch. After eight. They close at eight-thirty. Well, if I didn't catch them tonight I could catch them tomorrow. And if I did catch them tonight I'd check out a videotape myself. One that was all noise and flashing lights and simple straight-line plot and demanded no thinking at all. More like James Bond than *Agnes of God* or something you have to really think about. I just wasn't up to thought.

Besides that, I wanted my baby.

I thought, wistfully, of the old Rock Hudson-Doris Day movies. I took Vicky to one of them when she was a baby. In those days you could safely take children to romantic comedies without worrying about what they were going to see. I don't remember which one it was, I do know that it was several years old even then, but I remember that it had some sort of dream sequence in it that was all full of clouds and colored lights, and Vicky loved it. She cried like anything when the dream sequence ended and semi-reality returned. I had to take her out to the lobby, so I never did find out how Rock Hudson got Doris Day that time. Or how Doris Day got Rock Hudson, which was more often how it went.

Reality, Deb. Rock Hudson died of AIDS and Doris Day is an animal rights activist. I was just tired enough to see some elusive relationship there, but I was too tired to catch it, and it hovered around on the edges of my subconscious while I parked in the Sounds Easy parking lot.

The girl who worked there—Carla Montoya—was already heading for the door with a key in her hands, but when she saw it was me she nodded and let me slip in. The dismay on her face when she saw the tape would have been comical if the situation hadn't been so serious. "We tell people and tell people—" she began.

Hastily I interrupted. "It isn't mine. It's Dorene Coe's."

"Dorene Coe?"

"Do you know her?"

"Well, actually, yes I do. I used to go to high school with her. Were you on that case? I was so sorry to hear—but what do you mean? Dorene never checked tapes out here that I know of."

"Well, it says Sounds Easy, and she lives—"

"Let me see that," Carla said. Then she nodded. "I didn't think we had an overdue tape. This isn't ours."

"Isn't yours? But it says 'Sounds Easy'"

"I know, but Sounds Easy is a chain," she said unnecessarily. "Look." On the upper corner of the tape box was a strip of blue tape. I'd seen the big strip that said "Sounds Easy" but this one I'd missed entirely. It had a store number and an address in Arlington.

Arlington?

I took the box back and, for the first time, I looked at the title: *Indiana Jones and the Temple of Doom.*

Carla was right. This wasn't Dorene Coe's tape.

I had a pretty good hunch I knew whose tape it was. And tomorrow I was going to find out her name, and tomorrow I was going to close this case, and I hoped to goodness—though I knew how unlikely it was—that Lola Chavez was still alive to be rescued.

"Thank you," I said.

"Want me to get it back to them?"

"No, I'll take care of it," I said. "I will be very, very glad to take care of it."

· 10 ·

As I DROVE TOWARD home I was feeling considerably less sanguine. How could I assume that the blond would have used her real name to rent the tape, when she had used various assumed names for everything else? And I had been very excited by the fact that the video store was in Arlington, where Casavetes lives. But Casavetes and how many other people? Last I heard the population of Arlington was pushing two hundred thousand.

I went on thinking.

And by the time I turned onto my own street I was just about ready for a nervous breakdown, if there was just some way I could spare the time.

Because—was it the same team on Southwest Federal? No. It couldn't be. It could be one member of that team and somebody else.

That made sense if one of them was shot. You don't, at

least not generally, go out and rob a bank with a bullet in you.

The one who wasn't there could be Nick Casavetes because there wasn't a tall one and obviously if he was part of the team he had to be the tall one, except that if the tall one was the one who was shot then the tall one wasn't Nick Casavetes and I was barking up the wrong tree. And if it was the short one who was shot rather than the tall one then why was it the tall one was the one who wasn't there today?

Phil Casavetes, seen beside Nick, would look short, would give us our tall one and our short one. Phil Casavetes alone, or with someone his own height, would look average height, which would give us what we had today, except that if Phil Casavetes was one of the ones today that still gave me no explanation of how it happened that one of them was shot and it couldn't be either Phil or Nick.

Anyway I had no reason at all to suspect Phil Casavetes except that he was Nick's brother and, as Millner had pointed out to me, that really wasn't exceptionally fine reasoning. The only real reason I had to suspect Nick Casavetes was the expression on his face, and that wasn't a very good reason either.

So was either one of the ones today from the same team as the ones Saturday and Monday?

They used sawed-off shotguns. They took a hostage who was still missing. That sounded the same.

But they hit late in the afternoon, not early in the morning. And the best that I could determine they hadn't used a borrowed car. That didn't sound the same.

A copycat crime?

But they knew we were onto the borrowed-car thing—if they'd returned the last one (and where was it, by the way?) we'd have caught them.

The Lynx. The blue Lynx three people—so far—apparently had died over.

The Lynx, we had strong reason to assume, was no longer mobile. But we didn't know its license plate number.

We did know the license plate number of the white Chevrolet that our Harrison Ford fan took from Clean Harry's A-1 Used Cars. We were looking for that car. But we had no reason at all to be looking for a white Chevrolet that had a different license plate on it.

The Lynx's license plate?

It wouldn't work permanently. But it would certainly work for a while.

Instruct all the patrol officers to run a license check on every 1979 white Chevrolet they saw? Well, that would certainly clog the computer, but it might be necessary.

I went in the front door. No one was there. The back door was open and the playpen was on the patio; the not-so-sweet smell of mosquito goop mingled with the odor of barbecued chicken. Pat for once hadn't taken advantage of the open door to rush inside; he wasn't even salivating at the chicken. No, he was lying beside the playpen adoring Cameron, who should have been in bed hours ago but who seemed to be trying to figure out a way to put the moon in his mouth.

The picnic table had been returned to the backyard, and a bowl of salad was on it, covered by a dish towel. "Baked potatoes are in the oven," Lori told me, and immediately added, "I told Aunt Doris I had to stay over here late tonight because you had to work late and you were going to be tired."

This girl is becoming more and more alarmingly maternal. While I have no objection to her as a daughter-in-law, I hope she realizes how long it will be before Hal is ready to take on the responsibility of a family.

I hope Hal also realizes it.

Though I should be grateful. It was probably Lori who thought to put the mosquito goop on Cameron. If he'd been put outside at night without it none of us—especially not Cameron—would be sleeping tonight.

So I ate supper and played with the baby—at least, inadvertently as it might be, we seemed to be following Susan's recommendation to keep him up in the early part of the night—and waited for the inevitable telephone call to tell me Lola Chavez's car had been found in Trinity Park or some similar place.

The call came at nine-thirty, the car was in the parking lot of the Amon Carter Museum of Art (again, the same general area), and the patrolman was absolutely certain it had not been there thirty-five minutes earlier, because he'd stopped there to talk with a man who was having car trouble.

Which probably said something but I'm darned if I know what.

The problem was that the clues were all so very mixed up. The crimes, without exception, were either right downtown or in the general northeast Tarrant County area. I had strong reason, namely the rented videotape, to believe that at least the blond female lived in Arlington; that's west of Fort Worth, due west on the DFW turnpike. But the cars and the victims kept turning up in the southwest Fort Worth area, and that didn't make any sense whatever in relation to the rest of the case.

The southwest Fort Worth area, in places easily accessed off the west freeway.

Okay, you come in on the turnpike from Arlington and you turn north on 820 to go pull a robbery. Then you get back on 820 to go west, to dispose of the car and the body—

That didn't make any sense either. Anyway we were having more and more indications that the car and the body weren't being disposed of until after dark, which would mean they had to be holed up somewhere in the meantime, and anybody would be completely crazy to go driving up and down 820 with a body in the body's car knowing perfectly well there were lookouts on that car and that victim—

It didn't make any sense at all.

I know. I keep saying that.

If you were Nick Casavetes and you wanted to go from a bank on Belknap to a job in Euless you had to take the Airport Freeway and it's totally torn up right now—

By now I was hopelessly confused. Nick had definitely been at work at the time of the robbery on Belknap. He'd arrived at work Monday twenty-five minutes after that robbery, and that wasn't on Belknap, that was on Beach Street. And Beach Street to Glenview Drive is very, very, very easy if you know your back roads and don't try to do it on a main street.

Maybe that was the key. Because if you take Glenview Drive to Pipeline Road to Hurst Boulevard that'll run you right into Euless, and if you do that you *can* get from a bank on Belknap to a boat shop in Euless in twenty-five minutes if you don't care whom you run over and if Smoky doesn't stop you, and on those back roads you've got a medium good chance Smoky won't catch you.

"Penny for your thoughts," Harry said, and I shook my head. I was still sitting at the kitchen table with the telephone in my right hand and the baby on my lap.

What was the patrolman's stranded motorist driving? Was it a white Chevrolet?

What if it wasn't the tall one or the short one that was shot? What if it was the blond?

I knew Carlos Amado well enough to know he'd never have voluntarily shot a woman. But if a woman was shooting at him I figured he'd return fire. Most people would.

Still with the now-very-drowsy baby on my lap, I pulled out the phone book and started making telephone calls, on my nice convenient metro line.

To the Arlington Police Department. I asked them to go by the Sounds Easy at the address on the tape and find out the name of the emergency contact. Usually that's taped to an inconspicuous little card on the door. You call the emergency contact if the place has been burglarized, or if the burglar alarm is going off and won't stop and it's waking up the whole neighborhood.

"I can give you the emergency number," the dispatcher said, "but what do I need to send a car out there for? We keep 'em on file in the office."

"Oh," I said meekly. Well, how was I supposed to know? I never have been in dispatch.

She gave me two emergency numbers, the manager and the assistant manager, and I called them and they were both busy.

My idea was, if I could get the manager up there and we could at least check on who had rented the videotape, without waiting till morning, maybe we could get Lola Chavez back alive.

Kidding myself on that one? Of course I was. But on the other hand Deandra Black was still alive. Just barely, but she was alive.

What if it wasn't a tall man and a short man? What if this time it was a short man and a woman—the blond? Oh, we knew it wasn't on the first two robberies, because each time the blond had been seen letting the other two out of the car. But this time we didn't have any witnesses that had seen anything like that, and this time only one of the robbers had spoken. All sixty Cub Scouts agreed on that.

Well, fifty-eight of them. One of the other two insisted the robbers were Martians and one was too scared of cops to tell us anything.

I called back on the emergency numbers.

They were both still busy, and I had stalled just about as long as I could get away with and then some.

Calling Millner, I inquired the purpose of my going to the art museum. Sarah, I pointed out, could process the car without my assistance. There was, really, nothing at all there for me to see or do. I could be a lot more use on the telephone following up some ideas I had.

Millner did not agree. He told me so. At some length.

Surrendering my warm wet bundle to Harry, I went and put my shoulder holster back on and left for the Amon Carter Museum of Art, with the nagging feeling that there was something I should have done, somebody I should have called, that I couldn't think of.

Sarah Collins was hard at work when I arrived. A patrol officer—presumably the one who had found the car—was with her, semihelping but mostly watching and, presumably, protecting her from harm.

When I asked, the patrolman—his nametag said Dennis, which would be his last name, not his first—agreed that he had been the one who found Lola Chavez's maroon '87 Yugo. I congratulated him for spotting it and asked him what kind of car he'd been out with earlier.

"Earlier when?" he asked.

"When you were here before. Before you came back here and found the Yugo."

"Oh. Well, it was—now gee, what was it?" He pushed his hat back in a gesture that could have been painted by Norman Rockwell and said, "I guess it was a Chevy."

"What color? What year?"

"White. It could have been, oh, seventy-eight, seventy-nine, something in there."

"Did you fill out an FI card?"

He shook his head. "There wasn't any reason to. They were just having a little car trouble. I think it was flooded out. I jumped them off and they thanked me and left."

"'They' who?"

"What's this all about?" he asked belatedly. "Look, if you're thinking of that white Chevy Amado got killed over, that wasn't it. I checked the license plate. Of course I did."

"Did you run it?"

"No, I just looked at it and saw it wasn't the same."

"Do you happen to remember what it was?"

He shook his head, staring at me. "Are you saying they put a different plate on the car?"

"Wouldn't you?" I asked.

"Oh, hell," he said, in a tone more dismayed than the

rather conventional phrase would suggest. "Oh, hell. You mean I had—"

"You may very well have had."

"And I let 'em get away—"

"What did they look like, Dennis? Do you remember that?"

He shook his head. "Oh, a little. White male, white female. He had—in this light it's hard to tell. Darkish hair, maybe black, it was dark brown if it was brown. Just normal man's haircut. Not hippy or punk or anything. Eyes—I didn't even notice. No mustache or beard or anything like that. Medium height, call it five-seven, average weight. Jeans and a T-shirt. Age, I'd guess about thirty-five or so. Her—I'm sorry. I didn't even look at her."

"You don't even know if she was a blond?"

He shook his head again. "No. She was just—there. On the other side of the car. It was him I talked to."

It could have been a description of the short robber. It could have been a description of Phil Casavetes. It could also have been a description of any one of a million other men walking around the Dallas-Fort Worth metroplex.

Hypnosis, I thought. With hypnosis maybe we can get that license plate number out of him. He did look at it; he had to have looked at it, to know that it wasn't the right one. So it's in his head somewhere if we can just figure out a way to get it out.

But we can't do that tonight and this is Lola Chavez's Yugo and where is Lola Chavez?

Sarah crawled out of the Yugo holding one of the little white cards you tape lifted fingerprints onto, looking very pleased with herself.

"Same one," she said.

"Same one what?" I asked, reasonably enough in my opinion.

"Same print as I found in Deandra Black's car," she said.

"You can't have memorized it—" That wasn't true, of course. I've known a few people who could memorize some—not all—fingerprints, if they were searching those prints very hard. But it's rare.

"No," Sarah said, "but I can bring a photo of the prints with me, and I did. It was on the seat belt latch."

"Okay," I said, and then did a double take. "Wait a minute. I thought that was prints from the *right* hand you found in Deandra Black's car."

"It was. Right index, middle, and ring."

"So you found these prints on the passenger's seat belt?"

"Driver's seat belt."

"You found prints of the right hand on the driver's seat belt latch," I repeated, mentally going through the motions of latching and unlatching a seat belt. "That sounds awkward to me."

"It sounds awkward to me too," she said.

"You don't mean on that little piece that slips into the other little—"

"Uh-uh," she said firmly. "I mean on the part of the seat belt latch that you hold with your left hand. He left prints from his right hand on it. And yes, that sounds awkward. Very awkward indeed. The kind of thing that wouldn't likely happen—"

"Unless your right arm was a little out of commission," I said slowly. "So it wasn't the tall one Carlos winged at all—"

"It could have been," Sarah said.

"Oh. Yeah." Of course it could have been. Because if the tall one was the one Carlos winged then the tall one wouldn't want to be going into the bank, which would mean the tall one was driving the car that was at least the drop-off car if not also the getaway car or at least one of the getaway cars—

Which again meant it wasn't Casavetes.

I'd probably get a lot more work done if I'd mentally let go of Casavetes. But instead I found myself thinking about the position Casavetes—this was Nick Casavetes—had been in when I saw him. He was sawing something with a power saw. He was right-handed; I was sure of that. So could he have been using his left arm awkwardly and I just didn't notice because of the way he was standing?

Casavetes was turning into an obsession. Heaven knows every robbery series results in dozens, maybe even hundreds, of completely innocent cases of mistaken identity. I would have no trouble at all letting go of this one if it just wasn't for the expression on Casavetes's face every time he looked at me. That I'm-getting-away-with-it-and-you-can't-prove-a-damn-thing look. Every time I have seen that expression on somebody's face—*every* time without exception—the person has been up to something. And maybe it was just some little con he was up to, maybe he was going to be doing some kite flying—hustling checks back and forth between banks and milking them both with no money—but I didn't believe that because the kind of man who makes a Green Beret, if he decides to turn to crime, isn't going to be a con man. The personality is totally different.

I left Sarah working on the car and the patrolman guarding her—he didn't seem at all unhappy with the task—and went to look for Lola Chavez. Of course I was not the only one looking for Lola Chavez.

I did not find Lola Chavez. Neither did anybody else.

After it became evident that I had looked in all the places I could think of to look, I went back into the police station and pulled out our copies of the videotapes of the three robberies and I started showing them, over and over and over, noting everything I could think of about the three people.

I could not say any of the three was Nick Casavetes. I

could not say any of the three was Phil Casavetes. But also I could not say any of the three definitely was neither Nick Casavetes nor Phil Casavetes.

I could not say either of the short ones in the third videotape was female. I also could not say neither of them was female. One—the one doing the talking—was male. That was certain, and I was pretty sure he was the same one who had been the short one at my own robbery, but again I could not be sure.

On that I did not have to be sure. Once we got him some other way, voiceprints could tie him in to these two crimes.

I had no way whatever of judging whether the short one was Phil Casavetes. I had never heard Phil Casavetes speak. I had heard Nick Casavetes speak, but I could not say for sure the tall man was him. But here again, I also could not say the tall one was not Nick Casavetes.

Okay, look at the tapes again. See how tall the tall one is compared to me. That's easy. Why didn't I think of it sooner? I'm five-two. Look—

I'm five-two. He is not quite as much taller than me as Millner is. Millner is six-four. But the robber is taller than Harry is. Call him six-two. That's close. That's probably almost exactly on target.

Casavetes is six-two.

The short one looks about five-seven, which isn't really short, in fact it's just about right on the nose of average white male height in the United States. He just looked short compared to the tall one, which is what I figured.

Phil Casavetes is about five-seven.

Phil Casavetes was at work when the Monday robbery went down.

I stopped long enough to make notes of my musings, of my plans for the morrow, starting with going to the Sounds Easy in Arlington to find out who rented that *Indiana Jones* tape. Then I resumed musing.

Susan says at least one of the robbers hates women.

Some women hate women.

Was it the blond who pulled the trigger?

When Captain Millner came in at five A.M. I was asleep with my head on my desk. He woke me up and said, "Deb, go home."

"I'm okay," I said.

"The hell you're okay. Go home and get some sleep."

"I don't need to. I was just resting my eyes for a minute."

"You're the most argumentative broad in seventeen counties," Millner said. "Go home and get some sleep."

"Look, I've got a real good idea that I think is going to lead us to them—"

"I said—"

"But Lola Chavez's life is at stake—"

"Lola Chavez is dead," Millner said.

I stared at him. "When did they find her?"

"They didn't find her."

"Then how do you know she's dead? Deandra Black—"

"Was a fluke. We'll find Chavez today. Whatever your idea is you can tell me about it later."

"After they rob another bank? Take another hostage? Murder somebody else?"

"Deb, if your idea is that good, why didn't you check it last night?"

"Because I didn't get it until too late to check it out."

"Can you check it out now?"

"They don't open till ten," I said.

"Then check it out at ten. That's five hours away. Go home and get some sleep."

I freely admit that if I had been operating on all cylinders I would, right then, have picked up the phone and called those emergency numbers at Sounds Easy again. Undoubtedly I would have startled somebody out of seven years' growth, considering the time, but on the other hand

I could have gotten somebody down to the store right then to check the name on the overdue Harrison Ford videotape. But I was not operating on all cylinders; I was dead on my feet.

So I just left and went home.

Harry was sitting on the couch feeding the baby. He looked up at me and asked, "What time do you want me to wake you up?"

"Nine," I said, and went to bed with my clothes on.

And my shoes.

And my pistol.

· 11 ·

I snapped awake at seven-thirty, after only an hour and a half of sleep, with the realization that I had omitted a very important factor from my calculations. It was this: No matter how carefully they planned everything else, they did *not* plan for the Lynx to break down.

The man at the parking garage had been unclear as to exactly when the New Yorker had been removed, but it was at least an hour after the robbery. Was the New Yorker taken *because* the Lynx broke down? Mrs. Farmer was unclear as to exactly when the Lynx broke down in front of her day-care center, but she was sure it was before noon because the child—Scott—was left in her care while his mother took care of getting the car hauled away and getting a ride, and the records showed he'd been removed about eleven forty-five. Allowing time for the wrecker to come and get the Lynx and somebody to come and get the mother, that didn't leave much time at all after the robbery for the blond to go to the car lot (west of the bank) and retrieve the Lynx and then get back to the day-care center (considerably east of the bank) to retrieve the child.

But the mother arrived there alone. Mrs. Farmer was certain of that. If—as was almost certain—the blond had picked up the two robbers and the hostage after the robbery, then she must have dropped them back off somewhere else at another vehicle almost immediately thereafter. So if they already had another vehicle then why was a replacement for the Lynx essential?

Maybe they needed to go in several different directions?

Of course arguing against all that scenario was the fact that they had made Dorene take her car keys with her. But who is to know what is in the mind of a panicked bank robber? Maybe they wanted her keys just in case.

It was pretty obvious, though I suppose not completely certain, that the kidnapping of Dorene Coe was an afterthought. The other two abductions—I hoped it was still no more than two—were certainly planned. Perhaps so we'd go looking for the hostage's car instead of the robbers' car?

I washed my face and went into the living room. "I told you I'd wake you up at nine," Harry said in a rather annoyed tone of voice. He was sitting at the kitchen table doing things with papers it appeared he didn't want me to know about. At least not yet. I supposed he would tell me in his own good time.

"I couldn't sleep." I sat, rather limply, on the couch. "I'm going to Arlington."

"Dressed like that?"

"What's wrong with how I'm dressed?"

"It looks like you slept in your clothes, that's what's wrong with how you're dressed."

"That's because I did."

"I'm aware of that. You might as well go back to bed for another hour or so. If you're going to Sounds Easy you know they don't open till ten, so what's the use of scampering off at seven-thirty?"

"Maybe I can get them to open sooner." I telephoned the emergency numbers, which I had not thought to do early this morning, but there was no answer.

"Go back to bed," Harry said again. "I'll wake you up. Cameron's fine, you can see that."

Clearly Cameron was just fine. Harry had hung a prism in the window that opened onto the patio, and Cameron was trying to eat the resultant dancing rainbow.

"I can't sleep," I repeated.

"Then lie down on the couch and at least rest."

So I lay down on the couch and slept like a corpse for an hour and then got up, showered, ate the breakfast Harry badgered me into eating by taking my car keys and refusing to surrender them until after I had eaten, and then I left for Arlington, in the detective car I'd brought home at a quarter to six so that I could go straight to Arlington without having to go to the police department first.

It took me an hour and fifteen minutes to get to Sounds Easy. I spent thirty-five minutes of it waiting at that awful bottleneck where you exit the turnpike going right if you're coming from Fort Worth, going left if you're coming from Dallas—that's assuming you're going to Arlington, of course, which I was. My best time ever going through that intersection is twenty minutes and that was on a Sunday morning.

Why so long on a Sunday morning?

Well, there are two churches—large ones—very near, and besides that, the exit is the one you take to the Grand Prairie flea market. And then there are all the reserve bases for the weekend warriors—well, you get the picture.

Unfortunately there is no other good way to get to Arlington or Grand Prairie. When they built the turnpike they made it just about impossible to get over, under, or around it, and when they changed it from a turnpike to a freeway they didn't improve it any. Not in that regard.

Did I call my office and tell them where I was going? No. I did not. I had told Captain Millner at 5 A.M.—at least I thought I had; opinions on that matter varied, I learned later—and I didn't see that it was necessary to say the same thing twice. Anyway Harry was going to call Millner and remind him I was headed for Arlington. Besides all that I had my radio with me.

Turned off.

No, I was not operating on all cylinders. I already said that.

But I found the Sounds Easy store fairly easily. It was in a small shopping center; there was a little branch post office, and a grocery store, and a dime store, and a drugstore, and a frozen yogurt shop all scattered around, and not very many cars were there. Apparently ten o'clock is still considered awfully early to do much shopping.

I went in through the metal detection door—well, I don't think it's actually metal detectors though it looks like them; I think it's really some kind of system that causes magnetic tape to set off beepers, so that you can't exit with their tapes without them knowing it—and produced the tape and my badge.

No, I did not give them the tape. Not anymore. With my discovery that it had not been checked out by Dorene Coe, it instantly became evidence.

Boy, was it ever evidence. The clerk—a redhead named Larry Hampton—told me it had been rented by one Marla Casavetes. With very little urging, they looked through their records and located Marla Casavetes's address for me.

That was the point at which I should have called for help. That is what is wrong with operating on two hours or so of sleep—you don't remember when you should, or should not, ask for help.

I just drove over there.

Well, I was a little more cautious than that might

sound. I didn't go charging up and knock at the door, at least not at first. I looked to see if they were home. To be precise, I sat in the car parked on the street—I am *very* careful about not going in without search warrants—and looked to see what I could see.

What I could see was nothing of note. It looked like a perfectly ordinary, not expensive but not poverty row, suburban house. Probably three bedrooms.

Then I counted to see how many houses it was from the corner, and I drove around in the alley and stopped—again being careful to stay on the right-of-way—to see what I could see.

What I could see was a blue Lynx, cousin to my late unlamented vehicle. Its hood had been removed and its engine was dangling from a jury-rigged block and tackle. Apparently they had decided to try to fix the transmission themselves. I hoped they knew a lot about cars. When mine died Harry said trying to fix the transmission at home wasn't worth the trouble.

Then I wondered why they were bothering with it, considering the bank loot. Force of habit? Working off nervous energy?

Apparently this was one of those suburbs that requires garages at the back rather than at the front, and requires the garages to be closable. But closable does not mean closed. The door was wide open and there was no other vehicle visible.

I itched to look in the garbage can and see if there was any bloodstained gauze or anything like that, which might indicate home treatment of a bullet wound, but that was probably at this point illegal. I didn't have a search warrant. Besides that it might be futile. I had no way of knowing when garbage on this street was picked up.

I drove back around to the front, parked the car on the street again, told my radio where I was and wondered vaguely why the radio didn't answer, and went diddy-bopping up the walk to the front door, which if it is not the stupidest thing I have ever done in my life certainly doesn't miss it by far.

But I was fortunate. They weren't at home.

I was fortunate. It occurred to me that somebody else might not be so fortunate. So far they had pulled a robbery on Saturday, a robbery on Monday, and a robbery on Tuesday. This was Wednesday and if I were a bank teller in Fort Worth, I would be very, very nervous right about now.

Well, now what?

I could call Euless PD and tell them to go pick up Casavetes but I didn't have a warrant and at this point it would be somewhat less than legal to make an arrest without a warrant. Whatever I did, or caused somebody else to do, was going to be strictly legal. I did not want there to be a chance in the world that these killers would walk.

I could call Euless PD and tell them to have somebody go sit on Presto Boats to watch for Casavetes, but if he was there and started to leave and was stopped there was likely to be a bloodbath that could be prevented by a better choice of time and place. If he was not there and started to arrive and saw a police car or two or three he would keep right on going. So that was not such a good idea either, at least not right now.

Besides that I still did not know whether it was going to turn out to be Nick or Phil or both. And also I did not want to risk spooking the other one, or two, or however many it was, members of the gang.

The fact was that for everything I could think of to do there were strong reasons why that was not the thing I should be doing at this particular point in time.

If I could pick up the blond first—make sure she didn't have a chance to warn the others—maybe she'd be the one most likely to tell who the others were—

I drove back over to Sounds Easy and asked if they had any idea where Marla Casavetes worked. It might have been a silly question but who knows, they might need this information on their records before people rent tapes. I didn't know because Harry got our Sounds Easy card and all our other movie rental cards, of which we had quite a lot. Commercial TV is getting so tiresome even Hal doesn't watch it that much anymore.

To my surprise, but not much to my surprise, Hampton nodded without even going to pull out any of his records. "Yeah," he said, "she works right over there in the yogurt shop. I'd have told you awhile ago if I'd known you needed it. Usually she's there in the afternoon but Monday they hauled Eileen, that's the lady that's usually there in the morning, into the hospital with appendicitis and so Marla worked yesterday morning and I'm pretty sure I saw her opening up this morning."

And that explained it. That simple. Why they had changed their schedule on Tuesday—because Marla had to work at the yogurt shop in the morning.

So far they had taken about $300,000 all told from the three banks they had hit, but Marla had to work in the yogurt shop.

So what did I do?

Well, I didn't say it was the world's greatest idea. But it made sense to me at the time.

I went over to the yogurt shop and ordered a chocolate frozen yogurt from the straight-haired blond standing behind the counter. The blond was, maybe, ten years younger than I am, and from her appearance I'd say her nerves were pretty frazzled. She kept yelling at the child, who was romping around making the kind of racket a healthy child makes. "Scottie!" she screamed once. "Stop that right now!"

So he stopped. For about two minutes, and then resumed running in circles on the floor. She smacked him.

What did she expect him to do while she worked? She hadn't brought him any toys, any coloring books. Was he just supposed to sit quietly like a little mouse for however many hours it was she was working?

Okay. I was sure, now. I had traced the blond. This

was Melanie Griffith Carrie Fisher—Marla Casavetes—and that meant that at least one, and quite possibly both, of the Casavetes brothers were in on it. So I had to decide what to do now. What I had better do was get to a phone and call Millner and get started on arrest warrants. As soon as I finished my yogurt—I hadn't been this hungry for a long time, maybe knowing what was going on had done something good for my appetite—

And the door opened.

The front door opened and Nick Casavetes walked in and before I could get the yogurt spoon out of my hand and get to my pistol Nick Casavetes had a sawed-off shotgun pointed at me.

I do not like the north end of northbound shotguns. I especially do not like it when the south end is being held by somebody who's already killed.

"What the hell?" Marla demanded, coming around the end of the counter to stand beside him and stare at me.

"She's a cop," Nick said. "She's that smart-ass cop Phil and me've been telling you about." He walked over closer to me, so that the muzzle of the shotgun was right under my nose. "How'd you find out? Huh? How'd you find out?"

"It was real easy," I answered. "You really were casing the bank Monday, right?"

He shrugged. "So how'd you know?"

"I'll tell you if you tell me how you rigged the time clock."

"You're in a real great position to be bargaining."

I managed to shrug. "I saw Dorene. And Harry Weaver and Carlos Amado and Deandra Black. How can I get in a worse position than I already am? I'll tell you how I got onto Marla if you'll tell me how you rigged the time clock."

He grinned. "Rigged the time clock? Lady, you can't rig no time clock. I was there. Course I drove like a bat outa hell to get there, but I was there. It was Phil that was smart. He clocked in at seven fifty-five, same as always, and worked for half an hour and then went to the back of the lot and walked right back around to the front and got in the car with me. That stupid old man can't see his nose in front of his face; how was he going to know if Phil was there or not? So when we got back Phil went in the same way he went out and he was standing right there at the time clock to yell at me for being late. Now. Your turn." He wiggled the barrel of the shotgun at me.

Again I shrugged. "I got to her the same way my captain is going to, real soon, because I left the information on my desk. It was the tape."

"Tape? What the hell are you talking about?"

"*Indiana Jones and the Temple of Doom*. On the dash of Dorene Coe's New Yorker. Only Dorene didn't check it out. Marla did."

"You stupid bitch!" Nick Casavetes yelled, and backhanded Marla who slapped him back, shotgun or no shotgun. I thought maybe I could get out the door while they were fighting, but when I headed for it Nick swung back around again, the muzzle of the shotgun headed my way. "I wouldn't try it, lady," he said.

I don't think I have ever in my life been so totally devoid of ideas. I mean, last time somebody pointed a shotgun at me I vomited on his arm and grossed him out. But I was pregnant at the time. I wasn't sure I *could* vomit right now, and even if I could I was quite sure it would have no effect whatever on Nick Casavetes. Marla, maybe. But not Nick.

No. It would have no effect on Marla either—maybe less than it would on Nick. Marla now made her feelings plain.

"Well, shoot her!" Marla screamed.

"Not here," Nick said mildly.

"Then give me the gun and I'll—"

"I said *not here*," Nick repeated, still in a very mild and reasonable tone of voice.

The telephone shrilled, and he turned his head. "Don't answer it, Marla," he said.

"It might be the boss."

"Then tell her you was in the john. You don't need to worry about her much longer anyhow. We'll be out of here."

"It might be Phil."

"We'll pick Phil up in just a minute."

"Which one of you was hit?" I asked.

They both turned and stared at me as if I had gone completely mad, and perhaps I had, asking questions at such a time as this. But in the first place I really did want to know, and in the second place maybe if I could distract their attentions from this truly fascinating discussion as to where they were going to shoot me—

That is not as silly an idea as it sounds. At least it wouldn't be if Nick were drunk. I had once caught a drunk in the act of strangling his wife. As I was unarmed at the time, and approximately half his size, I could do nothing physically. So I asked him a question. He let go of his wife to answer me, and by the time he was through with the explanation not only had his wife escaped, but also he had forgotten what he was doing.

But Nick wasn't drunk and he didn't look very distractable.

"Aren't you going to tell me?" I asked.

"Me," he said. "That's what you were looking for, wasn't it, yesterday at the shop? I figured it was. He just winged me. Skinned my ribs a little. He paid for it." Nick Casavetes grinned slowly. "He paid for it. It took him awhile to die."

I would like for it to take Nick Casavetes awhile to die. *I would like to kill Nick Casavetes myself,* I thought. But at the moment that seemed quite out of the question.

"So that's why Marla went in on the last bank job, and you stayed in the car."

Again he grinned slowly. "I stayed at work. You think I didn't know you would check on me?"

"And that's not why I went into the bank," Marla said. "It was 'cause I wanted to. Just 'cause I wanted to. Same reason I shot Deandra Black. Same reason I shot 'em all. 'Cause I wanted to. I told Nick and Phil to bring me more bitches to shoot. Damn snotty women with their pretty clothes, looking down on me like I'm some kind of trash because I work in a restaurant—"

"Marla, I've worked in a restaurant," I said. "Nobody looks down on you because—"

"Oh, shut up!" she yelled. "You think you're going to talk me around on your side?"

Not one of us had spared a thought for the child, the four-year-old Scott Casavetes. Until now. Nick looked around. "Scott," he said, "open the lady's purse and get her gun out."

Scott trotted around staying out of the line of fire, which told me this was not the first time he had been involved in his parents' activities, and opened my purse. "It's not there."

Nick backhanded him without taking the muzzle of the shotgun away from me. "I said get it out, you little bastard!"

"He told you it's not there!" I screamed. "You idiot, don't you think he can see? I do not have a gun in my purse!"

"Then where is it?" He looked at me. "Shoulder holster. That's it. Shoulder holster. I should have guessed. A ball-breaking broad like you, she's got to have it in a shoulder holster. Scott, get it—"

"What's a shoulder holster?" the boy asked, not daring to sob despite the tears running down his dirty face.

"I'll get it out," I said. It wouldn't do me any good not to; if I didn't Nick would get it himself, after slamming the child around a few more times, and a shoulder holster isn't made to be opened by a four-year-old.

"Don't try nothing fancy," he said, and watched as I took the pistol out and laid it on the little ice-cream table in front of me.

"There," I said. "Satisfied?"

"Scott, get the gun and take it to your mom."

Marla grinned, that kind of self-satisfied grin that always makes me want to slap somebody.

"You don't shoot her until I say you can," Nick added hastily. "For cryin' out loud, Marla, use your head! You can't go shooting somebody here and now."

"Why not?" Marla asked sulkily. "She's already said they're onto us."

By now Marla had my gun. Maybe I could con her into using it on him instead of me. In tones of intense curiosity, I inquired, "Nick, does Marla know about Rita?"

Nick laughed. "You think you're making her mad, guess again. Marla's Phil's wife, not mine. Sure, Marla knows about Rita. Don't you, Marla?"

"Never mind that now, Nick," Marla said. "We've got to get out of here. Didn't you hear her say they're onto us?"

"If they're onto us how come she's the only one here?" Nick demanded. "Are you too dumb to tell a bluff when you see one?"

"It's not a bluff," I said. "I didn't bring backups because I wasn't planning on making an arrest yet, just doing a little investigating. But if you think I'd take off like this without telling Captain Millner where I'm going you're even crazier than I think you are . . . and does that sound like a bluff?"

Of course I was bluffing. I had left notes on my desk about the tape. There was about a twenty percent chance that Millner would sit down at my desk and read those notes. But the sounds on the street were timely.

"That sounds like fire sirens," Nick said.

He wasn't certain. But neither was I. Not until the three Arlington police cars entered the parking lot from three different directions and converged on the yogurt shop.

Clearly Millner *had* read my notes. And called Sounds Easy. And called the yogurt shop. And when the yogurt shop hadn't answered he'd gotten me backups. Fast.

But fast enough?

Because these people took hostages.

And right now I was the only possible hostage.

Whatever happened, I couldn't let them take me out that door.

Marla darted to the door. She picked up Scottie, holding him in front of her, and yelled, "Stay back!"

"Stay back!" Scottie dutifully echoed, not the least bit aware that his own mother was using him as a shield.

"Lady, get your car keys," Nick told me.

He—or Phil, I couldn't remember now which—had said those same words to Dorene Coe. I'd heard them. And probably to Deandra Black and Lola Chavez, although I hadn't been there to hear them. Now Dorene was dead. Deandra was in critical condition. And Lola? I didn't know about Lola.

"What happened to Lola Chavez?" I asked.

"What the hell do you think happened to Lola Chavez?" he asked. "She's behind the levee at Trinity Park, if nobody's found her yet."

"But you want me to walk out that door with you? What kind of a fool do you think I am?"

"What kind of a choice do you think you've got?"

"If you shoot me here at least I've got a chance. There are cop cars out there, probably an ambulance standing by."

"Which won't do you a hill o' beans of good if we won't let them in to get at you."

"But shooting me won't do you a hill of beans of good," I argued. "If you shoot me you're a dead man. They fry cop killers in Texas."

"Lady, I'm already a cop killer," Nick answered. "So it don't look like I got much of a choice. Neither do you. You die here and now or live a few hours longer, that's your choice. And you're just like everybody else. You'll go for the time."

If he was right then I had no choice. But he didn't have to be right.

There had to be a choice. I refused to allow there to be no choice. If he wanted to kill me he was going to have to do it my way, which would at least give me a little bit of chance and would certainly end his chances.

I couldn't vomit successfully, though I was pretty sure that given half a chance I could have diarrhea very successfully indeed. But I could sneeze.

I could fake a sneeze.

I sneezed, very loudly, and leaned over my purse. "Leave that alone," Nick yelled.

"I sneezed! Can't I get a Kleenex? You know I haven't got a gun in here."

"Get a Kleenex, then, but don't try anything funny."

True, I didn't have a gun in my purse. But I did have a pair of handcuffs, and handcuffs are far easier to hide in a wad of Kleenex than a gun is. I pulled out the handcuffs and, in best protesting female manner, and before Nick had time to yell, I handcuffed myself to the brass bar of the table.

Which was bolted to the floor.

"Unlock that," he shouted.

"I can't unlock it. I don't have the key on my key ring."

"Scott, get the lady's keys."

Were the uniformed police outside doing nothing while all this was going on?

Certainly not.

They were doing all they could do, which was stand around and wait. I was sure that the back door, if there was one, was blocked. I was sure their superior officers were on the way and that Captain Millner was on the way from Fort Worth. Probably a skilled hostage negotiator was on the way from Dallas.

That didn't alter the fact that I was sitting here handcuffed to a table inside a yogurt shop in the company of two people whose only disagreement about killing me was over the matter of when and where to do it. And if bullets started flying that question was likely to become moot. I was in the line of fire.

Scott found my keys and took them to Nick. And sure enough the handcuff key wasn't on the ring.

Now, notice I had not lied. I just hadn't told the whole truth. A few months ago, in New Mexico, I met a police chief who was absolutely brilliant at the art of lying by misdirection rather than by actual lying. I had *not* said I did not have a handcuff key. In fact I did have a handcuff key. I had just said it was not on my key ring. And it was not. It was behind a folded-in flap in the currency section of my billfold.

Nick Casavetes could not be expected to grasp such a distinction, especially when I did not wish to explain it to him. And he did not bother to ask.

Having backhanded Marla and Scottie, he now decided it was time to backhand me. This was not amusing.

Did I mention that I was sitting in front of a window? Yes, of course I did. So the police outside saw him slap me. Which was sufficient to let them know, if they did not know already, that he and I were not the closest of friends.

I honestly didn't know what I would do if I were the one outside, the one outside making the decisions. The rules for hostage negotiations are that you negotiate as long as possible, giving in on small points but never on large ones, and never, never, under any circumstances, do you allow them to depart with hostages. The only reason they had been able to before was because they had left before the police—or any police in decision-making positions, at any rate—had arrived.

So I knew I would not be leaving with them, whether or not they looked in my purse and found my handcuff key. What I did not know, what I had no way of guessing, was whether I would be leaving on my feet, or on a stretcher, or in a body bag. And right now there wasn't anything I could do about it.

At least nobody had started shooting. Marla was standing at the front door with my pistol, picking up Scottie often enough that the police outside could see there was a child inside and at least one adult who was prepared to use the child as a shield. She didn't say that, but she didn't need to. Her body language was eloquent.

Nick was pacing like a caged tiger. Three times already he'd checked to be sure the back door out of the store was locked; it still was, but of course there was always the possibility that they could contact the owner, get the key, and unlock the back door and come in while Nick and Marla were busy at the front.

Finally he got nervous enough that he stuck a chair under the doorknob. It probably wouldn't keep the door shut but it would make a lot of noise if anybody tried to open the door. Then he came back to the front, with the shotgun.

Oddly, the four-year-old wasn't scared. I guess he thought we were playing cops and robbers. And of course we were, but not in the way he thought we were.

Moved by some impulse I'd never in a million years be able to explain, I resumed eating my now half-melted yogurt. Nick gaped at me and then turned his attention back to the door. Actually it wasn't bravado. For some reason probably having to do with the metabolism of adrenaline, I was about as hungry as I had ever been in my life. If I could be turned loose now on a large steak, neither Harry nor Susan would have any reason to complain about my appetite.

The yogurt was gone and I had a pretty good idea nobody would bring me any more, no matter how nicely I asked. So I turned my attention back to the street. Still more cars were arriving. Dub and Chang. Millner. They must have blocked that crummy intersection; there was no other way Millner could have gotten here that fast, unless this episode had taken a lot more time than I thought it had.

The telephone began to ring. Nobody answered it.

"Casavetes!" somebody yelled from outside. "Answer the phone!"

Casavetes yelled back an obscenity and the phone went on ringing.

"Casavetes! You can't get out, so you might as well give up."

"I want a handcuff key and a police car and an hour's head start!" he shouted back.

"Why a handcuff key?" the voice outside asked, sounding genuinely curious.

"Because this bitch in here's locked herself to the table."

Millner scratched his nose. I could see him doing it. "What did you expect her to do?" he asked in his most reasonable voice. "She couldn't possibly leave with you."

"I'm not bargaining with you," Casavetes said. "In five minutes I start shooting hostages."

"Then what do you use to bargain with?" the negotiator asked.

"That's my problem. You get me what I asked for."

"But we're not going to get you any of those things," the negotiator responded, "because you'd kill your hostage anyway. You've already proved that."

Nick walked over to me and put the shotgun in front of my nose for a minute before he walked back to the front door. "So maybe she dies sooner," he replied.

I hoped there was a convenient bathroom. I was definitely going to need one if I got out alive. "Don't get your bowels in an uproar" is supposed to be a joke, but it was becoming less and less of one.

I don't know who made the decision. The negotiator shouted, "Tear gas coming in," and a tear gas shell lobbed right through the window—not the one I was sitting next to, but the other one—and the room began to fill with smoke.

"Nick, what are we gonna do?" Marla choked, already beginning to cough and wheeze. I could hear Scott crying, but I could barely see anybody. Of course I too was coughing and wheezing, and tears were rolling down my face. I had been tear-gassed before, and I was well aware the stuff was not called tear gas for nothing.

Without answering, Nick turned and dashed for the

back of the building. Was he going out the back door? Did he really not realize there were police outside the back as well as outside the front?

But I was wrong. He didn't go for the door. He opened the door of the walk-in freezer and ran inside, with Marla right behind him. The door slammed behind them. Neither had given a thought to the screaming four-year-old frantically trying to find the door.

Did they think the air was better in there?

Was the air better in there?

How long did they propose to stay in there and what did they expect to do when they got out?

I didn't much care.

Wiping my streaming eyes, I managed to get my billfold open and my handcuff key out. I unlocked the handcuffs but kept my billfold in my hand so that I could display the badge as I went out the door.

Then I headed for the freezer and snapped the outside latch on it before picking up Scottie, yelling, "Don't shoot, I'm Detective Ralston," and going out the door with Scottie in my arms and my badge displayed in front of him.

· Epilogue ·

I *DIDN'T* NEED TO go to the hospital. There wasn't the least reason for me to need to go to the hospital, just because I'd breathed a little tear gas. I'd breathed tear gas before. But the EMTs said things about shock—I wasn't in shock, I was just *cold* for cryin' out loud.

At least Millner didn't make me ride in the ambulance and he didn't send—or take—me to the closest emergency receiving hospital. He asked Chang, of all people, to drive my car back to the police station, and put me in his car and took me to John Petersmith Hospital in Fort Worth, chewing me out every inch of the way for not taking a backup with me or sending for one and waiting around till it got there. In vain did I point out to him that there was no reason I should need a backup when I was just going to look at somebody who had never seen me before and wouldn't know me from Adam. He just kept telling me I ought to have better sense.

All right. I ought to have better sense. Can we talk about something else now?

The emergency room doctors checked me over and said some more things about shock and told me they were admitting me overnight.

I said a few regrettable things and Millner left to go call Harry. He came back and told me Harry wasn't home and all he'd gotten was my answering machine, which Harry, who is crazy about gadgets, had bought just before the helicopter crash and hadn't hooked up until last week.

I didn't know where Harry was. Also by now I was a tad woozy because they had shot me full of antihistamines, which were supposed to help counter the effects of the tear gas. I hoped something would. Last time I got a good dose of tear gas I had bronchitis for six weeks.

Sometime about eight o'clock—at night, that is—I woke briefly to find a man standing beside my bed. "Are you Deb Ralston?" he asked.

"Uh-huh," I said. "Why?"

"I'm Don Black," he told me. "Deandra Black's husband. They tell me you found her. That if you hadn't insisted on going and looking for her she wouldn't have been found till the next day."

"Well, maybe—"

"The doctors told me if she'd laid out there another half hour she'd have bled to death. Now they say she'll be okay. So I just wanted to thank you. That's all. I just wanted to thank you. I'm sorry I woke you."

"You didn't wake me. I was awake anyway."

But maybe I wasn't awake anyway, because I slept again and this time when I woke up Harry was there. He didn't have the baby with him—you aren't supposed to bring babies into the hospital to visit because they might get all sorts of germs—and he was looking very pale. But he didn't fuss at me. I guess he knew it wouldn't do any good.

"You know all those papers I've been hiding from you?" he asked me.

"Uh-huh," I said. "And I haven't tried to read them."

"I know you haven't, and that's nice of you. Well, this afternoon Cameron and I took them over and delivered them. I'll be starting into management school next Wednesday."

"That's nice," I said, and went back to sleep.

They let me go home the next morning, and Captain Millner told me that reports or no reports, he didn't want to see me back at work for two more days.

Good grief. Do they think I am a petunia? They weren't nearly this nice when I shot that guy last September, and this time I didn't have to shoot anybody and all I got was a little tear-gassed.

Well, and slapped once.

May Rector from three houses down dropped by—she's a nice old lady who goes to Hal's church—and after giving me some poppyseed cake and playing with Cameron for a while, she said, "You know, I never go anywhere in the evening anymore. It sure would be nice if you'd let me come over and stay with this pretty baby when you have to go to work in the evening."

"Well, I was trying to find an on-call baby-sitter," I began, "but—"

"Oh, dear, no, not as a baby-sitter!" she said emphatically. "Just as a friend. It would be so nice. I know you get called out a lot and sometimes your husband and son just aren't convenient—and I do love babies so much—and I know your baby has a grandmother but she doesn't live as close as I do—"

Anybody who can do you a favor while making it appear you are doing them a favor has to be seen to be believed. I suspected I was going to be getting to know May Rector a lot better over the next two or so years.

That night on the news there was something complicated that I couldn't understand—but Harry listened closely, because it was covered in the textbook for his first course, and he already had the textbook and was reading it—about deficit spending.

"Deficit ending," I said during the commercial.

"What?" Harry said, looking at me.

"Deficit ending," I repeated. "Nobody won. They didn't win because they got caught. But we didn't win by catching them because we still lost Carlos—and all those other people who lost people, Dorene and Lola and Harry Weaver—and that poor little Casavetes boy, his mother was ready to let him get killed—everybody lost. And I don't have any more milk and I have to feed Cameron just bottles. *Everybody* lost, Harry."

"Well," Harry said, "I think you had better go back to sleep."

"I don't want to go to sleep."

"Then what do you want to do?"

"Harry," I said, "I'm hungry."